MW01145009

Issues in
Crime

Other books in the Contemporary Issues series:

CONTEMPORARY ISSUES

Issues in
Crime

by Patricia D. Netzley

Lucent Books, San Diego, CA

Library of Congress Cataloging-in-Publication Data

Netzley, Patricia D.
  Issues in crime / by Patricia D. Netzley.
    p. cm.—(Contemporary issues)
  Includes bibliographical references and index.
  Summary: Examines aspects of the American criminal justice system, including police powers, gun control, mandatory sentencing, juvenile justice, and the death penalty.
  ISBN 1-56006-480-3 (alk. paper)
    1. Criminal justice, Administration of—United States—Juvenile literature. 2. Crime—United States—Juvenile literature. [1. Criminal justice, Administration of.] I. Title. II. Contemporary issues (San Diego, Calif.)
HV9950.N48 2000
364.973—dc21   99-044980

TABLE OF CONTENTS

Foreword

When men are brought face to face with their opponents, forced to listen and learn and mend their ideas, they cease to be children and savages and begin to live like civilized men. Then only is freedom a reality, when men may voice their opinions because they must examine their opinions.

Walter Lippmann, American editor and writer

CONTROVERSY FOSTERS DEBATE. The very mention of a controversial issue prompts listeners to choose sides and offer opinion. But seeing beyond one's opinions is often difficult. As Walter Lippmann implies, true reasoning comes from the ability to appreciate and understand a multiplicity of viewpoints. This ability to assess the range of opinions is not innate; it is learned by the careful study of an issue. Those who wish to reason well, as Lippmann attests, must be willing to examine their own opinions even as they weigh the positive and negative qualities of the opinions of others.

The *Contemporary Issues* series explores controversial topics through the lens of opinion. The series addresses some of today's most debated issues and, drawing on the diversity of opinions, presents a narrative that reflects the controversy surrounding those issues. All of the quoted testimonies are taken from primary sources and represent both prominent and lesser-known persons who have argued these topics. For example, the title on biomedical ethics contains the views of physicians commenting on both sides of the physician-assisted suicide issue: Some wage a moral argument that assisted suicide allows patients to die with dignity, while others assert that assisted suicide violates the Hippocratic oath. Yet the book also includes the opinions of those who see the issue in a more personal way. The relative of a person who died by assisted suicide feels the loss of a loved one and makes a plaintive cry against it, while companions of another assisted suicide victim attest that their friend no longer wanted to endure the agony of a slow death. The profusion of quotes illustrates the range of thoughts and emotions that impinge on any debate. Displaying the range of perspectives, the series is designed to show how personal belief—whether informed by statistical evidence, religious conviction, or public opinion—shapes and complicates arguments.

Each title in the *Contemporary Issues* series discusses multiple controversies within a single field of debate. The title on environmental issues, for example, contains one chapter that asks whether the Endangered Species Act should be repealed, while another asks if Americans can afford the economic and social costs of environmentalism. Narrowing the focus of debate to a specific question, each chapter sharpens the competing perspectives and investigates the philosophies and personal convictions that inform these viewpoints.

Students researching contemporary issues will find this format particularly useful in uncovering the central controversies of topics by placing them in a moral, economic, or political context that allows the students to easily see the points of disagreement. Because of this structure, the series provides an excellent launching point for further research. By clearly defining major points of contention, the series also aids readers in critically examining the structure and source of debates. While providing a resource on which to model persuasive essays, the quoted opinions also permit students to investigate the credibility and usefulness of the evidence presented.

For students contending with current issues, the ability to assess the credibility, usefulness, and persuasiveness of the testimony as well as the factual evidence given by the quoted experts is critical not only in judging the merits of these arguments but in analyzing the students' own beliefs. By plumbing the logic of another person's opinions, readers will be better able to assess their own thinking. And this, in turn, can promote the type of introspection that leads to a conviction based on reason. Though *Contemporary Issues* offers the opportunity to shape one's own opinions in light of competing or concordant philosophies, above all, it shows readers that well-reasoned, well-intentioned arguments can be countered by opposing opinions of equal worth.

Critically examining one's own opinions as well as the opinions of others is what Walter Lippmann believes makes an individual "civilized." Developing the skill early can only aid a reader's understanding of both moral conviction and political action. For students, a facility for reasoning is indispensable. Comprehending the foundations of opinions leads the student to the heart of controversy— to a recognition of what is at stake when holding a certain viewpoint. But the goal is not detached analysis; the issues are often far too immediate for that. The *Contemporary Issues* series induces the reader not only to see the shape of a current controversy, but to engage it, to respond to it, and ultimately to find one's place within it.

Introduction

The Rights of Individuals Versus the Rights of Society

THE UNITED STATES WAS founded on the principle that personal freedom is essential to a democratic society. The nation's Constitution ensures that people have the right to express their opinions and practice the religion of their choice without fear of oppression. This protection of individual rights is also at the heart of the criminal justice system, which mandates that every person is presumed innocent until proven guilty in a court of law and that police must follow carefully prescribed rules and procedures while investigating a crime.

Because of such rules, if police officers suspect a person of being a drug dealer, they cannot search that person's home for proof of their suspicion until they have gathered enough evidence to convince a judge that a search is warranted. Without that warrant, a search would be illegal, and any evidence gathered in that search would be unusable in court. This ensures that individuals are free from harassment by representatives of the government—in this case, the police.

Protecting Society

Although individual rights are the foundation of American life, they are not the only rights that govern the nation. Society as a whole also has certain rights. For example, the government has the right to exercise authority so as to maintain public order and protect citizens

9

*Individual rights, such as the right to refuse a police search without a
warrant, sometimes clash with societal rights.*

from physical harm. The most famous example of this right is the
prohibition against yelling "fire" in a crowded theater unless the fire
is real. A prank of this nature might cause innocent people to get
hurt during the subsequent panic; therefore the government can
restrict free speech to ensure public safety.

In other words, when safeguards that protect individual rights
infringe upon societal rights, they are curtailed. Preventing unwar-
ranted panic is in the interests of society, so individuals are not
allowed to incite a riot. Sometimes, however, individual rights are
protected at the expense of societal rights. For example, if police are
unable to search a criminal's home because they do not have a warrant, that criminal might go free. Society therefore loses on two
counts: first because the lawbreaker has escaped punishment from
breaking the rules of society, and second because the absence of
consequences emboldens others to commit similar crimes.

As Diane Whiteley, who studies issues related to criminal justice and ethics, points out, laws exist to send a message to the community at large that crime will not be tolerated and to verify that
victims have rights too. She explains:

[Criminal legislation tells] members of society which types of actions are forbidden. It has the socially beneficial aim of deterring crime. . . . When a crime is committed, . . . it is through punishment that victim and community express their outrage at the victim's being devalued.[1]

Crime expert James Q. Wilson draws a parallel between expanding individual rights and an increase in crime, suggesting that the same freedom that encourages personal expression also encourages self-indulgence. In other words, a person who feels free to do whatever he or she wants might also feel free to commit crimes. He says:

The most significant thing in the last half-century [in America] has been the dramatic expansion in personal freedom and personal mobility, individual rights, the reorienting of culture around individuals. We obviously value that. But like all human gains, it has been purchased at a price. Most people faced with greater freedom from family, law, village, clan, have used it for good purposes—artistic expression, economic entrepreneurship, self-expression—but a small fraction of people have used it for bad purposes. So just as we have had an artistic and economic explosion, we have had a crime explosion. I think the two are indissolubly entwined.[2]

Reducing the Rights of Individuals

Because of this connection, some people have suggested that individual rights be reduced in order to reduce crime. To this end, various proposals have been made to make it easier for police to detain, search, and question suspects. For example, Judge Harold Rothwax, in his book *Guilty: The Collapse of Criminal Justice*, argues that the Fourth Amendment, which gives people the right to be free from "unreasonable searches and seizures,"[3] should not be interpreted to mean that evidence discovered by a police officer without a search warrant has to be excluded from a trial. He says, "The Fourth Amendment does not state that illegally obtained evidence must be excluded. We've come to that point entirely on our own."[4]

Some people assert that police officers should be allowed to use items obtained in a search as evidence against a criminal in court.

However, Rothwax adds that he is not saying police can barge into private homes without just cause—merely that laws need to be relaxed so that evidence found coincidental to a search can still be used against a criminal in court. As an example, he cites a case where police had a search warrant to look for evidence related to a bombing incident and instead found material proving that the suspect was a pornographer; however, the U.S. Supreme Court later disallowed this evidence and overturned the man's conviction because the search warrant said nothing about looking for pornography. Therefore, Rothwax says,

Few would disagree that in the United States, police officers should not be allowed to just burst into your home, or search your car, or rifle through your handbag on a whim. Such behavior would betray our fundamental right to be protected from unreasonable government interference with our lives. But we've gotten ourselves into a hopeless morass with the Fourth Amendment. Day by day, case by case, the results become more ridiculous and more difficult to understand and predict. The bottom line: Criminals are going free.[5]

Preventing Abuse

Other people, however, believe that even the smallest curtailment of individual rights will lead to abuses. In the case of searches, for example, they maintain that if laws are relaxed so that anything found "accidentally" during a search can be used as evidence in court, then police will find ways to make such "accidents" more likely to occur.

Even Rothwax acknowledges that care must be taken to keep such abuses from happening, to ensure that Americans continue to live "in a democracy, not a police state." He points out that "the entire thrust of our Bill of Rights is to restrain governmental power and, ideally, to allow it to operate effectively, without oppression and abuse."[6] However, few people agree on the way to achieve a balance between government power and individual power. How do lawmakers determine when a particular individual right is so harmful to society that it must be curtailed? Conversely, how do they decide that an individual right is so important to the principles of a free society that it must be protected at all costs? What aspects of the criminal justice system need to change, and to what extent? There are no easy answers to these questions.

Chapter 1

Should the Powers of Police Be Diminished?

IN 1990, TWO SIXTEEN-YEAR-OLDS, Philip Lewis and Brian Willard, were riding double on a motorcycle in Sacramento County, California, when a police officer directing traffic by hand signaled them to stop. Instead they kept going, and when a second officer began pursuing them by car, they accelerated. The police chase continued at speeds of up to one hundred miles per hour, down several residential streets and through four stop signs; along the way a bicyclist and some cars were almost hit. The chase ended when the motorcycle skidded out of control, throwing Lewis into the path of the police car. He died at the scene. Meanwhile, Willard ran away but was later caught and convicted of felony hit-and-run driving because of his friend's death.

But Lewis's parents were not satisfied with this result. They blamed the police chase for their son's death and sued Sacramento County for their "deliberate or reckless indifference to life" in conducting this chase. Their case went all the way to the U.S. Supreme Court, which held the police blameless because they were just doing their job. The Court said that as long as a high-speed chase was "aimed at apprehending a suspected offender"[7] it could be conducted without subjecting the government or the individual officers to lawsuits if someone gets hurt during that chase.

Lewis's parents protested this decision, saying that the Court was being unfair in putting society's rights ahead of individual rights. They stated, "It's a very sad day for all the innocent victims of these pursuits. The Supreme Court . . . has made a choice to protect the rights and privileges of law enforcement while abandoning

14

innocent citizens."[8] Moreover, their attorney called for lawmakers to limit the right of police to chase suspects.

Limiting Police Chases

Many others have also called for such limits. For example, journalist Sam Newlund, in an editorial for the *Minneapolis Star Tribune,* says, "Surely, it's time to consider banning police chases altogether, except in the most extraordinary circumstances." He believes that such chases should not be sanctioned by society because "the risk of injury or death—to innocent bystanders, to the suspect and to the officers themselves—is too great to justify hot pursuit for the sake of hot pursuit."[9]

Statistics indicate that there is indeed a significant risk of injury involved with high-speed chases. Estimates on the number of people injured during a chase, whether involved in the chase or innocent bystanders, range from fifty-five thousand according to a group called Solutions to Tragedies of Police Pursuits (STOPP) to a quarter million according to an August 1998 article in the *Denver Rocky Mountain News.* Estimates on the number of people killed during

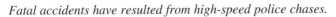

Fatal accidents have resulted from high-speed police chases.

police pursuits range from four hundred people a year according to the National Highway Traffic Safety Commission to twenty-five hundred a year according to STOPP.

The difference between four hundred and twenty-five hundred deaths is significant, but some people argue that numbers are unimportant, because even one needless death is too many. For example, political activist Barbara Dority, in discussing the Lewis case, says:

> In an on-line discussion I encountered shortly after the ruling [regarding Lewis's parents' lawsuit] was released, a police officer wrote: "When someone decides to step on it [i.e., speed] instead of stopping, I have to decide whether this is worth an innocent getting killed over." What? I was stupefied. Sometimes it's okay for public servants and protectors to take innocent life? And they get to decide when? Let me be very clear: I, for one, never agreed to give law enforcement the power to take such actions or make such decisions, and I never will. Instead of deciding if the apprehension of a particular suspect is worth the death of an unknown innocent, police should ask themselves which one of their loved ones they'd be willing to sacrifice. How about their parents? Their wives? Their children?[10]

The program director of STOPP, Jeffrey Maceiko, agrees with this position, pointing out that "more people are killed each year in a high-speed police chase than by an officer's gun, making the police car, like the gun, truly a weapon of deadly force."[11] Consequently he believes that police pursuits should be reserved only for people who flee major crimes, such as bank robbers. Some cities have heeded such suggestions. For example, in 1992 Miami, Florida, adopted the policy that police would only chase people fleeing from the scene of a major crime. As a result, in the year following the enactment of this new policy, police chases went down 82 percent, with a corresponding decrease in chase-related accidents.

Eroding Police Authority

To some, limiting society's right to pursue criminals is a positive change, because it might protect the lives of people like Lewis. The

Proposals that limit police pursuits are aimed at reducing the risk of accidents.

sixteen-year-old would never have been pursued—and consequently killed—under a policy like the one in Miami, because he was not fleeing a major crime and had no record of committing major crimes in the past. (He was, however, on probation for a previous theft and had been ordered to stay away from his friend Willard, which is perhaps why the two fled police.) Supporters of Miami's policy also point out that fewer chases mean less risk to innocent bystanders who might be struck and killed during a police pursuit.

But other people fear that society will ultimately suffer for giving individuals the chance to avoid pursuit. For example, in discussing the Miami policy, sociologist and criminologist Richard Moran says,

> Restricting chases to fleeing felons under favorable road conditions is a sensible short-term strategy, but I wonder what the long-term results will be. The conventional wisdom is that effective law enforcement requires the police to give chase. If drivers realize the police will not pursue,

more of them will decide to make a run for it, thereby endangering the public and further eroding police authority and effectiveness.[12]

Many police officers agree that curtailing their ability to pursue people who flee their command to stop, for whatever reason, will hamper their ability to protect society. For example, former officer Paul Linnee says,

> Many think that policies or laws need to be enacted to curb or prohibit police from engaging in such chases. That is society's right. But it needs to be understood that limiting the authority of the police to pursue persons who flee will, inevitably, mean more people will elude capture. That's more repeated drunk drivers (who may kill again), . . . more persons fleeing from a crime scene, etc.[13]

Maceiko counters that a driver fleeing police need not escape punishment simply because the police decide to end the chase, since officers can find out the address of a car owner via the car's license plate. He suggests that the alternative to a pursuit is simply to note the license number and arrest the driver later. However, Linnee says that there is no way to prove that the owner of the car and the driver of the car are the same person. Therefore, he explains,

> merely knowing who the registered owner of a car is does not mean that the owner can be successfully prosecuted for whatever the [criminal did]. It's not like parking [tickets], where the registered owner is always responsible. One needs to be able to ID the original driver and place that driver behind that wheel at that time on that date.[14]

The Realities of Police Work

Linnee believes that police must be allowed to do their jobs in the way they see fit, and that catching people "who will do darn near anything to avoid capture" is part of that job. He further complains that the public wants good law enforcement yet will not face the realities of police work. He says:

Although police chases can have devastating outcomes, too many restrictions may hamper law enforcement's ability to do its job.

Cops generally become cops with the initial primary intent of "catching bad guys." And I think that's still what the public wants them to do. Catching bad guys is sometimes analogous to making sausage. Folks often like the outcome, but they don't really want to see and know the intimate details of the process.[15]

Part of that process requires police to make split-second decisions involving complex situations. They must weigh their duty to protect society against the rights of individuals—and this includes their own rights as well. Police work is not only difficult but also dangerous, a fact that the U.S. Supreme Court specifically acknowledged in considering the Lewis case. Their ruling spoke of a police officer's "instinct"[16] to do his job and the fact that an officer cannot be faulted when his motive is to enforce the law. California attorney general Dan Lungren expressed a similar view in court papers related to the case, in which he pointed out that officers in the field must make quick decisions that cannot adequately be judged "in the reflective quiet of the courtroom."[17]

However, because the events leading up to and during a chase are so fast paced and so tense, decisions surrounding that chase can be flawed. This can lead to abuses of individual rights that some people believe are more dangerous to society than a few uncaptured suspects. As journalist Sam Newlund reports, chases involve "an adrenaline rush . . . [that] would make it difficult for anyone . . . to let the bad guy get away."[18]

Therefore Newlund believes that with every chase comes the risk that a police officer will assault the fleeing suspect once that suspect is finally caught. He explains that during a pursuit,

> the police officers have put themselves in danger, and they've bottled up barrels of adrenaline, energy, anger and fear. In California, some fleeing [criminals] were said to have hurled beer cans at their pursuers. At the end of that kind of chase, cops are bursting with steam to blow off. And if an officer is unskilled in handling such frustration—and if he happens to be bigoted against blacks or Mexican aliens or some other group to which the suspect belongs—look out."[19]

Police Abuse

In fact, in October 1998 a human rights group called Amnesty International reported that in some cases the police do engage in serious abuses related to capturing suspects who resist arrest. Some people therefore argue that the potential for police abuses mandates the enactment of tougher restrictions on police behavior. The proposed restrictions include not only the curtailment of chases but also restrictions on how much force a police officer can use during an arrest.

Those who favor restricting police powers often support their position by citing the case of Rodney King, one of the most famous instances of alleged police brutality in America. On March 3, 1991, after a long high-speed chase, police officers in Los Angeles, California, pulled King from his car and beat him repeatedly with a baton when he would not lie down on the ground. Their actions were captured on videotape by a local resident, and when the tape was aired on television, the public was outraged. Most people viewed the beating as either excessive or unnecessary.

*Rodney King's treatment at the hands of Los Angeles police gained
national attention.*

However, the officers insisted that the tape was misleading.
They and other officers have suggested that the public often per-
ceives brutality when in fact the police are using reasonable force
based on their own perception of the situation. New York police officer Juan Carlos Ramos offers a common example of how such mis-
perceptions come about:

> We get a description of a male carrying a gun. So now our
> adrenaline is flowing, and the only one who is going to
> arrive is myself and whoever my partner is. . . . We don't
> know if this person is going to shoot us. And now going
> back to the perception of civilians. They don't know why
> we are going there. We race to the scene. We have our guns

drawn. We put the guy against the wall or on the floor for our protection and everybody else's protection. We find out that it was a bogus phone call, but all the people see is police were harassing this innocent man. They don't know that we were responding to a phone call that this particular person was carrying a gun.[20]

The officers in the King case also experienced this rush of adrenaline, and they too believed that their suspect was dangerous. Consequently they felt their actions were appropriate given the threat that King posed and the tools they had available to make King lie down. In addition to the baton, they employed a device called the taser (a type of stun gun), which shoots an electrically charged copper wire onto a suspect from a distance of up to fifteen feet.

Controversial Weapons

The use of tasers and other types of stun guns, all of which deliver electric shocks to suspects by various means, is extremely controversial. Although they were originally developed as a nonlethal alternative to guns, some people believe that society should not have the right to use them on individuals because they are a cruel form of punishment. According to Amnesty International executive director William Schulz: "An eight-second shock invariably throws the prisoner to the ground and incapacitates him for up to 15 minutes. The person often will defecate or urinate on himself. It is pretty gruesome."[21] Therefore in October 1998 Amnesty International called on police departments to stop using such devices.

In fact, many departments have already stopped relying on stun guns, not because of public criticism but because the devices have proved ineffective. Law enforcement experts Samuel Faulkner and Larry Danaher of the FBI report:

When applied, [such devices] often leave burn marks on subjects and are not, in fact, effective in many situations. The Rodney King [beating] incident represents perhaps the most widely witnessed failure of any tool used to control a single subject. King could not be subdued immediately, despite repeated taser applications and baton blows. Police officers across America could relate similar, but less publicized, incidents.[22]

Moreover, Faulkner and Danaher argue that police should not be taught to rely on any weapon, lethal or nonlethal, during arrest situations. They state, "The perfect tool for controlling subjects does not exist and probably will not be discovered in the foreseeable future. Until that day, officers should be trained to rely on their own abilities with the aid of equipment—rather than relying on the equipment itself—to control resistive subjects."[23]

In other words, according to these experts, the key to good law enforcement lies in well-trained police, not more sophisticated weapons, and in fact many communities now agree with this view. They have enacted policies to reduce the risk that police in stressful situations like high-speed chases will become agitated enough to kill someone out of anger or other emotions rather than out of necessity. As Georgette Bennett, in her book *Crime Warps: The Future of Crime in America*, reports:

> The growing recognition of the misuse of deadly force by police and the wrenching stresses under which they must work is leading to an array of changes in police procedure: restrictions on use of firearms; psychological monitoring and removal of guns for burnt-out cops; ethical training in the consequences of deadly force; substitution of guns with nonlethal alternatives; and early warning systems to detect troubled police and intervene before they hurt themselves, their families, fellow officers, or the public.[24]

However, too much concern over the emotions and actions of police might also be detrimental to society. Studies suggest that when police worry about whether they are behaving properly—particularly in regard to whether they are adequately protecting an individual suspect's rights—they are less likely to capture the suspect and more likely to be hurt themselves. In the February 1998 issue of the *FBI Law Enforcement Bulletin*, law enforcement experts Anthony Pinizzotto, Edward Davis, and Charles Miller report that while studying incidents where officers got hurt on duty, they found that,

During the assaults, the officers in the study generally recalled what not to do and when not to use force, but some had difficulty recalling when the use of force was an appropriate, timely, necessary, and positive decision. Some had problems recalling their agencies' deadly force policies and determining when to progress to the next level of force, and many officers experienced great difficulty recognizing the point at which they actually were fighting for their lives.[25]

In other words, when officers were too self-conscious of their actions, they could not respond quickly enough to save themselves from harm. Therefore by restraining police with too many rules, society runs the risk of endangering officers' lives.

Increasing Police Powers

If police must be limited during arrest situations, some argue that they should also be given greater latitude during criminal investigations, in order to maintain some balance between individual and societal rights. This seems to be the view of the U.S. Supreme Court in recent years. The Court has begun to grant police greater powers

in search-and-seizure situations, making it easier for them to capture criminals. For example, in one case the Court supported a Minnesota police officer who looked through some window blinds, saw three people packaging drugs, and then went inside to arrest them. Prior to this ruling, unless an officer had just cause to believe that someone inside a house was in imminent danger, that officer could not spy on the occupants through a window and then use information received in that way to make an arrest.

As a result of this decision and others, law professor Alan Rafael says, "We've seen an erosion in individual liberties and an increase in government power in relation to search and seizures. This court almost always finds the balance weighing in favor of the government."[26]

The supporters of more relaxed search-and-seizure laws believe that such laws benefit society because they enable police to obtain more evidence against criminals. But human rights advocates worry that allowing the police more freedom to initiate a search and seizure of evidence will lead to serious abuses of individual rights. They argue that the Fourth Amendment was created specifically to limit police power and fear that worse abuses will stem from an erosion of constitutional protections.

Society as the Representation of Individuals

Most people agree that certain protections are necessary to keep innocent people from being subjected to an overzealous police force. However, society is obligated to keep innocent people from being subjected to criminal behavior as well. The problem is that society often has difficulty distinguishing the innocent from the guilty; therefore even a law-abiding citizen might falsely be accused of a crime. For this reason, as defense attorney Leslie Hagin explains,

> the fundamental thing that the Constitution seeks to do is to protect individuals from the enormous power of the state to deprive them of life, liberty, or property. . . . It is there . . . to protect all people, including people who are sometimes victims of crime, from being a victim of overzealous state

action or becoming another type of victim, a . . . wrongfully accused or wrongfully convicted person.[27]

Arguments over how to proceed with criminal investigations are therefore similar to those related to police chases, in that they revolve around the importance of protecting the rights of both criminals and innocent bystanders while trying to uphold society's right to enforce its laws. There must be a balance between concern for the accused and concern for the criminal justice system, because unless society can effectively safeguard its citizens, those citizens will find their rights curtailed—by criminals rather than by the government.

Chapter 2

Should Society Restrict Access to Guns?

D URING THE 1997 TO 1998 school year, there were five school shootings in five different small towns. In October 1997, a sixteen-year-old shot and killed nine students in Pearl, Mississippi. In December 1997, a fourteen-year-old shot and killed three students and wounded five in West Paducah, Kentucky. In March 1998, two boys shot and killed one teacher and four students in Jonesboro, Arkansas. In April 1998, a fourteen-year-old shot and killed a teacher in Edinboro, Pennsylvania. In May 1998, a sixteen-year-old shot and killed his parents, then shot and killed two students and wounded twenty-two others in Springfield, Oregon.

In April of the following year, two gun-toting high-school students in Littleton, Colorado, killed twelve students and a teacher before shooting themselves. This event, combined with previous school shootings, intensified the efforts of gun control advocates to limit access to firearms. They believe that violence in America would be reduced if society made it more difficult for individuals to obtain guns. U.S. Representative Charles Schumer of New York expressed this view at a May 1998 news conference when he said, "If these kids didn't have guns available to them, there wouldn't have been the mayhem in Springfield, Oregon. I would never have heard of the place."[28]

The idea of reducing gun violence appeals to most people. Achieving that goal by restricting access to firearms, however, does not have that level of support. Restrictions are viewed by many Americans as a violation of the constitutional right to own a gun.

Students comfort one another during a candlelight vigil held in honor of the fourteen students and one teacher killed at Columbine High School in Littleton, Colorado.

The Second Amendment

The Second Amendment to the Constitution states that civilian gun ownership is "necessary to the security of a free state." There is much disagreement over whether this necessity still exists today. The framers of the Constitution created the Second Amendment in part because they feared that an oppressive government might some-day take away their newfound freedom. Whether this could still happen in modern times is a matter of debate. Some people dismiss the notion as paranoid, but others argue that it is foolish to take American freedom for granted. Sylvia Kinyoun, a constituent of

California assemblywoman Hannah-Beth Jackson, expressed this sentiment in a letter protesting Jackson's proposal to register guns:

> There are those in this country who want every privately held gun registered with the federal government. To what purpose? So that somewhere down the road all of these guns can be confiscated? If that happened, who would be left with guns? The military, various federal agencies, and the criminals, who have the most [guns]. . . . Freedom isn't free; it requires responsibility and diligence.[29]

Under this view, the right to keep and bear arms is so important to a free society that it should never be curtailed. The counterargument is that the right to keep and bear arms is damaging society by making it too violent. Both sides in this debate are convinced that their position—either opposition to gun control or support for restricted gun ownership—will be best not only for society as a whole but for the individuals within that society. Moreover, both sides of the debate appear inflexible in their positions, and finding

Gun advocates cite the Second Amendment to the Constitution as the foremost guarantee of their right to bear arms.

legal and political compromises is difficult. As Ray Suarez, former host of the National Public Radio program *Talk of the Nation,* explains,

> We as a people seem unwilling or unable to have a nuanced conversation about universal access to firearms. No matter what outrageous acts are committed with these instruments, no matter how high the death toll, no matter how high the number of injuries and accidents, there seems a stake in describing these precise, brilliantly engineered, sophisticated machines as being utterly benign and placing all the burden on people. On the other side of the equation, there seems to exist an equal motivation to remove human agency from the use of firearms in this country in favor of concentrating on the implements themselves, as if they have a will of their own.[30]

In other words, some people blame crime and violence on the existence of guns, while others blame them on the people who use guns. The first group believes that restricting gun ownership will benefit society by making it more difficult for one person to shoot another for whatever reason. The second group believes that such restrictions trample individual rights; they suggest that the solution to violence lies in teaching people how to use guns responsibly and in dealing with criminals more forcefully.

Background Checks

Despite strong opposition, those who want to restrict gun ownership have made some headway in achieving their goals. Several laws have been enacted to set conditions for gun ownership and to limit what types of guns can be sold. The first major law in the United States limiting gun ownership was the Gun Control Act of 1968, which created a list of categories of people who are not allowed to buy or own firearms. These include people convicted of crimes and people who have a history of mental illness. The Gun Control Act put the FBI in charge of keeping records on such people, but it did not make it necessary for gun dealers to check such records before selling someone a gun.

In 1994, the Brady Handgun Violence Prevention Act was enacted to change this situation. Also known as the Brady Law, it was named after James Brady, once the press secretary to President Ronald Reagan, who was shot and seriously injured by a gunman attempting to assassinate the president. In its original form, the Brady Law required people purchasing a handgun to wait five days

The Brady Law was named after former presidential press secretary James Brady, who was injured in the attempt on President Reagan's life.

before receiving that gun, during which time their backgrounds would be checked at the state level for records of criminal behavior, domestic violence, court-mandated restraining orders, or mental instability.

In November 1998, the Brady Law was expanded to include all firearms, not just handguns. The new law also eliminated the mandatory five-day waiting period, which was replaced by a nearly instantaneous nationwide background check using a federal database. Because of sophisticated technology, a gun purchaser can be cleared or refused within minutes.

However, the instantaneous background checks must draw on an incomplete database. Felony conviction records are easily available at the federal level, but other information is not. Twenty-eight states have laws against accessing mental health records, eight states do not keep track of domestic abuse convictions, and three states cannot provide information about court-ordered protection or restraining orders. The Brady Law does not require these states to provide such information to the FBI.

The absence of a complete database prevents any real chance of success for the procedures set out in the Brady Law, says Sarah Brady. Brady is the wife of Jim Brady and the chairperson of Handgun Control Inc., the nation's largest citizen's gun control lobbying organization. She wants state and local governments to give the federal government even more access to information about individuals' backgrounds, arguing that "Without access to these databases, background checks on firearm purchases will never truly be complete."[31] Brady also believes that gun owners should be subjected to a minimum seventy-two-hour waiting period before receiving their guns. She reasons that this will give the FBI time to do a more thorough background check on each buyer and provide a cooling-off period for someone who is buying a gun in anger or distress.

Brady's proposals inconvenience gun purchasers, but they do not prevent a law-abiding citizen from buying a gun. Instead they merely give government agencies time to weed out those whom society has declared should not own guns. Nonetheless, there has been strong resistance to the idea of waiting periods and the use of a national database, on the grounds that taking away even part of an

individual's rights—to purchase a gun on demand—will lead to more serious limitations on individual rights in the future.

A Threat to Freedom

In fact, many gun control opponents see each new restriction as being another step down a path towards banning guns altogether. Jacob Sullum expressed this view in an editorial opposing a 1994 ban on a type of firearm called an assault weapon. After Congress passed a law that made it illegal to manufacture nineteen specific models of these semiautomatic weapons, Sullum argued that the ban would not only be ineffective in reducing crime but also that this ineffectiveness would be used to promote even stricter bans. He said:

> Gun-control activists will use the points made by the ban's critics to argue for more sweeping restrictions. They will note that the ban has not had an observable effect on crime. They will discover that it leaves untouched many guns that are just as dangerous as "assault weapons," if not more so. And they will already have established that it's OK to violate the right to keep and bear arms, as long as you have a reason. It doesn't even have to be a good one.[32]

MIKE SHAPIRO

"When your Grandma Constance and I were your age, we didn't have automatic weapons."

To Sullum, there was no good reason to ban assault weapons because they are not the weapon of choice for criminals and because they are no more dangerous to society than any other gun. He explains:

> Despite the scary-looking, military-style features, the guns are no more lethal than hundreds of firearms that remain legal. They fire at the same rate as any other semiautomatic gun—in other words, no faster than a revolver. Their ammunition is of intermediate caliber, less formidable than the cartridges fired by many hunting rifles.[33]

Moreover, the ban prevents only nineteen specific weapons from being manufactured or imported to the United States, and it does not ban the resale of such firearms. Assault weapons already in use in America at the time of the ban were exempt from its influence. Therefore, despite the ban it is still possible for an individual to obtain one of these weapons—and that is exactly what Eric Harris and Dylan Klebold did before shooting students at Columbine High School in April 1999. One of their guns was the Tec-9 assault weapon specifically listed in the ban.

Because of such incidents, some people believe that both new and used weapons should be banned, and not just by model but by broad category. For example, Josh Sugarman argues that all assault weapons and handguns should be banned:

> We can continue to push legislation of dubious effectiveness. Or we can acknowledge that gun violence is a public-health crisis fueled by an inherently dangerous consumer product. To end the crisis, we have to regulate—or, in the case of handguns and assault weapons, completely ban—the product.[34]

Sugarman believes that the Brady Law and other means of regulating ownership are not working well enough or fast enough to reduce violence caused by certain categories of guns, particularly handguns. Therefore, he says,

> Gun-control advocates cannot afford to spend . . . years battling over piecemeal measures that have little more to offer than good intentions. We are far past the point where registration, licensing, safety training, background checks, or waiting periods will have much effect on firearms violence. Tired of being shot and threatened, Americans are showing a deeper understanding of gun violence as a public-health issue, and are becoming aware of the need to restrict specific categories of weapons.[35]

Ignoring Existing Laws

However, Harris and Klebold found a way to obtain weapons despite existing laws. It is illegal for anyone to sell a gun to a minor, yet the two boys were able to find people willing to help them acquire guns. Moreover, they easily found a banned weapon through the resale market. With over 200 million guns now in private ownership in America, it would be very difficult to keep one individual from selling a weapon to another. Even if these private transactions were made illegal, criminals would still be able to obtain banned guns because they would ignore such laws.

This is the case in Jamaica, where the gun control laws are among the strictest in the world. Despite laws restricting what kinds

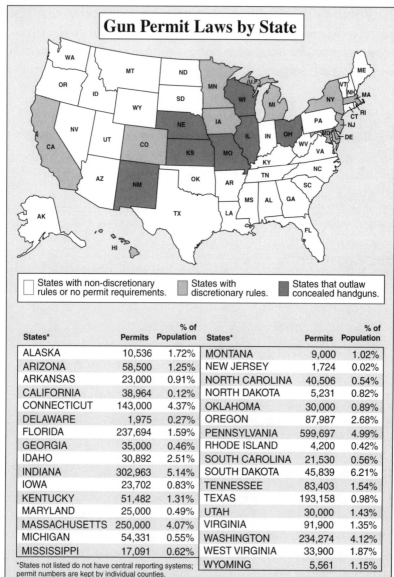

Gun Permit Laws by State

States with non-discretionary rules or no permit requirements.   States with discretionary rules.   States that outlaw concealed handguns.

States*	Permits	% of Population	States*	Permits	% of Population
ALASKA	10,536	1.72%	MONTANA	9,000	1.02%
ARIZONA	58,500	1.25%	NEW JERSEY	1,724	0.02%
ARKANSAS	23,000	0.91%	NORTH CAROLINA	40,506	0.54%
CALIFORNIA	38,964	0.12%	NORTH DAKOTA	5,231	0.82%
CONNECTICUT	143,000	4.37%	OKLAHOMA	30,000	0.89%
DELAWARE	1,975	0.27%	OREGON	87,987	2.68%
FLORIDA	237,694	1.59%	PENNSYLVANIA	599,697	4.99%
GEORGIA	35,000	0.46%	RHODE ISLAND	4,200	0.42%
IDAHO	30,892	2.51%	SOUTH CAROLINA	21,530	0.56%
INDIANA	302,963	5.14%	SOUTH DAKOTA	45,839	6.21%
IOWA	23,702	0.83%	TENNESSEE	83,403	1.54%
KENTUCKY	51,482	1.31%	TEXAS	193,158	0.98%
MARYLAND	25,000	0.49%	UTAH	30,000	1.43%
MASSACHUSETTS	250,000	4.07%	VIRGINIA	91,900	1.35%
MICHIGAN	54,331	0.55%	WASHINGTON	234,274	4.12%
MISSISSIPPI	17,091	0.62%	WEST VIRGINIA	33,900	1.87%
			WYOMING	5,561	1.15%

*States not listed do not have central reporting systems; permit numbers are kept by individual counties.

Source: Mike Miller/ The Salt Lake Tribune, 1999.

of guns can be in the country and who can use them, criminals continue to obtain weapons, and violence has escalated. In fact, in July 1999 the situation became so serious that the government decided to use the military to seize guns from private citizens. Prime Minister Percival Patterson announced that

The military will engage in a scientific search [using x-ray equipment] in the communities that we have identified as being the most volatile. If we are to have a significant reduction in the level of crime and violence, the primary targets have to be the guns and ammunition and the gangs which peddle them.

When asked whether this decision was related to politics based on public demands for drastic measures, Patterson replied, "We are not concerned about politics; we want the guns in. Wherever they are, we must find them."[36]

It will be a difficult task for the Jamaican military to confiscate all the guns in their country, and it would be impossible to do so in America. Criminals will always have guns—and criminals, say gun control opponents, are the real problem, not their weapons. As Richard Feldman, president of the American Shooting Sports Association, explains:

> The problem isn't the gun, the problem is in whose hands are the guns? If a million people own a million guns and don't misuse them, we don't have any problem. And if only a thousand people own a thousand guns, and they're criminals or they're irresponsible individuals, we have a huge problem.[37]

Addressing Criminal Behavior

To some people, then, the way to reduce crime is not to eliminate guns but to deal more effectively with criminal behavior. College student Scott Burger shares this opinion in a college newspaper:

> Since law-abiding citizens have a right to bear arms, guns will always be available. Therefore, what needs to be controlled is the will to commit criminal acts, not firearms. Making guns illegal will not reduce the crime rate. A person willing to murder another human being is not going to say, "Oops, this gun is illegal, I guess I can't shoot you with it." If we want to reduce the crime rate, we need to do it with common sense laws that attack criminals—not the tools they use.[38]

Burger believes that dealing more harshly with criminals is the key to reducing violence. Talk show host Sean Hannity agrees, arguing that someone who is intent on doing harm will always find a way to achieve their goals. He states,

> You cannot legislate that people be moral. . . . Let me tell you, you ban guns, are you going to ban gasoline, fertilizer, ammonia [which are used to make explosives]? Are you going to stop plumbing supply shops from selling pipes . . . [because] people build pipe bombs? The bottom line is, anybody with an evil intent in their heart [will kill].[39]

Some people apply this same argument to disturbed children, saying that students inclined to shoot classmates would kill their peers even without guns. For example, Paul Braun, who wrote to a newspaper to oppose new gun control proposals, says,

> Some people think that all of society's problems, which are caused by people's deliberate behavior, can and should be cured by passing laws and regulations. . . . [The politicians who pass these laws] are put into power by voters who believe the promises they make; who want to be taken care of like little children; who are willing to give up their freedoms for the imagined safe haven of a controlled and regulated society. I don't believe in that . . . [and know that] more laws restricting firearms would not have stopped the tragedy in Littleton, Colorado. Laws cannot control a heart that is lost in despair, bent on destruction.[40]

Safe Storage

However, gun control advocates use the same point—that disturbed people are not easily deterred from committing violence—to argue in favor of making firearms less accessible to law-abiding citizens as well as criminals. Students who shoot at schoolmates do not get their weapons from criminals. Instead they get them from family members, friends, and other people in their everyday lives. A 1998 study by the New Center to Prevent Handgun Violence showed that in nearly 40 percent of shootings committed by a child, the gun was owned by a

Many shootings committed by children might have been avoided had their parents been more careful about storing their firearms.

member of their immediate family, with an additional 7 percent owned by family friends. (In the remaining cases, the gun either belonged to the shooter or came from an unknown source.) The study also showed that when the guns of family members or friends were involved, 63 percent of the shootings could have been prevented had the guns been stored out of reach of children.

Because gun owners can be careless about gun storage, several state governments have been considering laws that would require manufacturers to put trigger locks and other safety features on their guns. A trigger lock prevents the gun from firing unless certain

Mandatory trigger locks have been suggested as a way to prevent accidental shootings.

devices are activated first, making the act of shooting more compli-cated for children. One state has already enacted a trigger-lock law. In October 1998, Massachusetts passed a law mandating the sale of a safety locking device with each firearm purchase and requiring adults to store guns out of the reach of children. The Massachusetts law also requires each gun owner to have safety training, bans the sale of certain types of guns, and increases penalties for those who disobey gun laws. It is therefore considered the strictest gun control law in the nation.

Many people opposed to mandatory waiting periods typically oppose mandatory trigger locks as well. For example, Congressman Earl Blumenauer of Oregon reports that in 1998 the National Rifle Association (NRA) convinced Republican politicians to fight all proposals related to gun safety features. He states,

> A year ago, the NRA and the Republican leadership decided they wouldn't even let us vote on the trigger lock legislation. . . . We wouldn't deal with gun violence in the

juvenile crime bill, and the word was, the NRA and the Republican leadership would not allow any vote in the remainder of this Congress.[41]

The most common argument against trigger locks is that they make it too difficult for someone to use a gun in self-defense. For example, John Lott, a professor at Yale Law School, says,

You can go ahead and . . . [enact] a gun lock rule, and you can penalize parents who don't lock up their guns. But you have to realize, that may make it so that guns aren't accessible to use to defend oneself . . . you're going to lose lives because parents aren't going to be able to defend themselves.[42]

Lott argues that the ability to defend oneself is an important individual right, and that society should therefore make guns more, rather than less, accessible to law-abiding citizens. In his book *More Guns, Less Crime*, Lott further suggests that arming the general public would reduce violence. He reasons that if every customer in a bank, for example, were carrying a gun, a robber would be less likely to try to rob it. Lott explains:

In all the research that I have done on crime control, there is only one measure that has succeeded in reducing deaths and injuries from these public shootings—letting law-abiding citizens carry concealed handguns. I did not support arming citizens when I began to study this. But I found that I had emotional reasons that were not based on facts. The ability to defend yourself is a potent weapon. Criminals don't want to get hurt. The possibility that they can be injured—and you let them know it—gives you an advantage.[43]

An Inviolable Right

Lott's contention that increasing gun use will decrease violence is not prevalent. Nonetheless, some gun control opponents do support his position, and many agree with his argument that an individual's right to keep a gun for self-defense is inviolable. Congressman Bob Barr, a Republican from Georgia, believes that the purpose of the Constitution is to protect individuals from government interference,

Many Americans believe that guns are necessary for self-defense.

and that therefore no constitutional amendment should be changed based on the political climate at any particular time in history. He states:

> Millions of law-abiding citizens cherish their Second Amendment right to keep and bear arms, a personal right explicitly guaranteed in our Constitution. No amendment to the Constitution, including the First Amendment, which protects free speech, the press and religious expression, is qualified with caveats saying, "Sometimes these rights will be withheld because of a particular political agenda."[44]

But gun control advocates counter that society does have the right to impose limits on human behavior whenever this behavior threatens the universal good. For example, as Bob Schwartz, executive director of the Juvenile Law Center in Philadelphia, Pennsylvania, explains, "We . . . have the right in society to try to find ways to limit [usage of potentially harmful products]. We do that, for example, with cars . . . we regulate driving. Cars are a deadly instrument. . . . [So] we don't let kids have access to them 'til they're 16 with a learners permit."[45] Therefore, Schwartz argues, gun use should be limited as well.

However, the Constitution does not explicitly state that people have a right to drive cars—and therein lies the reason that gun control debates become so passionate. The Constitution is one of America's most important documents, and many people believe that tampering with it is an assault on the principles of freedom. Individual rights outlined in the Constitution are deemed vital to the health of the nation. Yet school shootings and other acts of violence never imagined by the Constitution's framers continue to threaten American society's well-being, and so far no one has found a satisfying way to address these problems.

Chapter 3

Should Children Who Murder Be Treated as Adults?

O N OCTOBER 29, 1997, eleven-year-old Nathaniel Jamal Abraham allegedly shot eighteen-year-old Ronnie Lee Green Jr. while Green was coming out of a store. According to police, Abraham was two hundred yards away from Green, on a hillside near the store, when the shooting took place, and after firing the gun he ran home. Police had no idea who might have killed Green until two days later, when a neighbor reported that Abraham had shot at him earlier on the morning of the killing.

When police arrested Abraham, the boy confessed to the crime. Later, however, Abraham and his attorney, Daniel Bagdade, insisted that the death was an accident. They said that Abraham had been target shooting and hit Green by mistake. Nonetheless, Abraham was charged with murder and a judge ordered him to stand trial as an adult rather than a child because of the seriousness of the charge. This meant that if he was found guilty, Abraham could be sentenced to life in prison without parole, a punishment not used on children.

Therefore the decision to try Abraham as an adult created an immediate controversy. Some people were uncomfortable with the idea of sentencing a young boy to spend the remainder of his life in prison. But others argued that his crime was so heinous that it deserved the most severe punishment society can give. To these people, society's right to enforce its laws outweighs the rights of individual juvenile offenders; otherwise, social order will dissolve into chaos. Representative Charlie Weaver of Minnesota expresses this view when he says:

44

If we tell teenagers that they are not to blame when they beat or rape someone, or that real consequences will not follow from such crimes, we should not be surprised if they take us at our word—and rob, rape or murder their neighbors. Accountability and personal responsibility are long overdue; it is a vital part of our effort to reduce crime.[46]

Rehabilitation

This position marks a change in thinking from the traditional approach to juvenile crime. Since 1899, when the first juvenile court was established in the United States, the American justice system has treated young criminals differently from adult criminals, under

Eleven-year-old Nathaniel Jamal Abraham (pictured) was tried as an adult because of the seriousness of his crime.

the reasoning that young people are more malleable than adults. In other words, children are more easily led astray and therefore cannot be held wholly responsible for their crimes. Moreover, they are more easily rehabilitated and therefore can be taught to live law-abiding lives after only a short time in jail. Judy Briscoe, an expert on juvenile crime, expresses this view when she says:

> People must understand that the development of children and youth is a process that allows for learning, growing, changing, and maturing. Just as youth are vulnerable to negative influences, they are just as likely to be amenable to positive influences if adults can figure out how to reach them, or recognize they must be reached.[47]

Many people who work with juveniles support the idea that young criminals deserve counseling rather than harsh punishment. Some also suggest that society, rather than the criminals themselves, is to blame for juvenile crime. For example, James Gabarino, an expert on human development who has studied the behavior of

Some people assert that juvenile criminals should be counseled rather than punished.

young criminals, says that society has failed to offer troubled children the support they need to avoid a life of crime. He states:

> One of the striking things . . . is how often, how terribly often you can see in their childhood by the time they're eight- or nine-year-olds a discernable, definable mental health problem that isn't addressed well at all. We're still only responding with professional intervention to something like a third or a half of kids with identifiable mental health problems in childhood. And it's very clear that overwhelmingly kids who end up killing or committing very severe acts of violence come from that population. . . . That puts a different slant on this idea that these are just kids who show up and turn bad. They come out of a long period of developing problems and they're typically troubled kids whose experience has not been a positive one and has culminated in these terrible events.[48]

A Troubled Youth

In fact, Nathaniel Abraham clearly had signs of being a troubled child long before he shot Ronnie Green. In the two years prior to the murder, he had been in trouble with the law on twenty-one different occasions, suspected of committing crimes such as burglary, assault, and threatening to shoot a classmate. Seven of these accusations were made in the two weeks prior to Abraham's arrest; the most serious were related to his being named a suspect in the beating of a sixteen-year-old and a fourteen-year-old with a metal pipe. He was never found guilty of any of these crimes, but many experts believe that the number of accusations was a warning sign that Abraham needed serious counseling.

Although the court did send Abraham to an activity program for boys after he threatened to shoot a ten-year-old six months prior to Green's death, no other help was provided. Therefore, attorney Linda Bernard, an advocate for children's rights, says,

> This is a tragedy [not only] for Ronnie Lee Green and his family, [but also for] Nathaniel Abraham and his family, for you, for me, for our entire society. This should never have

happened. . . . We must intervene early, at the first sign of trouble, not after other children and adults have been injured or killed. We must fund and support social services and their work with families, which are key to prevention efforts."[49]

Bernard is referring to social programs that determine when a child is being abused and/or neglected and help families improve their living conditions. Many child advocacy groups point out that child abuse is strongly linked to juvenile crime. In several studies of condemned juvenile offenders, most had previously suffered repeated physical abuse and many had also been sexually abused by relatives.

There were no reports, however, of abuse in Abraham's home, and his attorney did not use this defense in his trial. Instead, he argued that no young offender, regardless of upbringing, can be held accountable for his or her actions, because children simply do not understand cause and effect. In other words, a child might not be able to foresee that playing with a gun could cause someone to get killed. Bagdade says, "Nate is 11 years old. Eleven-year-olds in our society don't understand the consequences of their actions.[50]

Knowing Right from Wrong

Many experts in human development share the view that children cannot grasp the full impact of their actions. Children might know that it is wrong to kill, for example, but they might equate this caveat with rules like "always wash your hands before dinner"—in other words, as something only mildly important and easily forgotten. Therefore, according to a *Time* magazine article on juvenile crime, while

> most psychologists agree that young children can grasp very basic concepts of right and wrong well before adolescence . . . most also say those concepts aren't well developed for kids under 10. . . . Seven-year-olds for the most part have little or no understanding of . . . higher-order concepts necessary to turn right and wrong into Right and Wrong—most significantly, death and remorse.[51]

Such immature thinking can lead children to draw incorrect conclusions regarding what their actions might mean to another human being. For example, psychiatry professor Carl Bell, who often counsels troubled urban youngsters, reports that children "know people die, but they don't know what it means. I've talked to seven-year-old kids who think when you're dead, you're just hanging out with someone."[52] However, attorney David Gorsica, who prosecuted Abraham for Green's murder, did not feel that such an excuse should be made for the defendant in his case. He states, "I believe Nathaniel knows the nature of his consequences. He knows the difference between right and wrong."[53]

Gorsica is convinced that Abraham intended to kill someone that day, not only because his previous behavior included threatening to kill a ten-year-old but also because of his actions on the day of the murder. According to Gorsica, just prior to the incident Abraham told friends that he was going to shoot someone, and afterwards he bragged to them about the murder. Moreover, according to witnesses, Abraham was not shooting at inanimate targets, but specifically aiming to kill. In a television interview, Gorsica describes the events of that day not as an accident but as a planned event:

He went over to a neighbor's home and stole a rifle. He also stole some ammunition. . . . He was shooting in the backyard. A neighbor came out. A bullet whizzed by the neighbor's head. . . . [Abraham] then went to a party store and perched on a hill . . . and basically was a sniper and waited for somebody to come by. He fired a shot at these three individuals entering the store. He missed. He waited for them to come out. He fired another shot and hit the victim in the head, killing him.[54]

Growing Violence

A jury agreed that Abraham acted deliberately rather than accidentally, finding him guilty in November 1999 of committing second-degree murder. This makes Abraham one of a growing number of children who commit murder each year. Between 1985 and 1995 the number of such homicides perpetrated by juveniles tripled from less than one thousand to more than three thousand. In 1996, 20 percent of all people arrested for serious crimes in the United States were juveniles; of these, 6 percent were under fifteen years old. In fact,

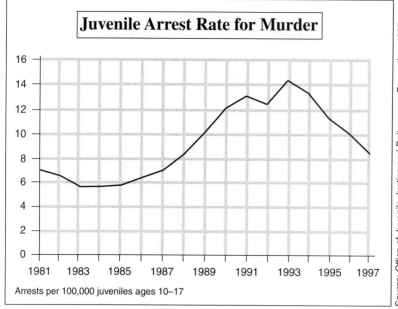

Juvenile Arrest Rate for Murder

Arrests per 100,000 juveniles ages 10–17

Source: Office of Juvenile Justice and Delinquency Prevention, 1998.

over thirty thousand children under fifteen were arrested for a variety of serious crimes, including murder, attempted murder, assault, and armed robbery.

Faced with growing violence among young people, the American public has increasingly supported the idea that society's right to protect itself from crime supercedes any concerns related to a juvenile criminal's youth. Many states have lowered the minimum age at which a child can be tried as an adult. Traditionally this age has been eighteen, although in the early 1990s many states reduced it to fourteen or fifteen. But recently Indiana, South Dakota, and Vermont lowered it to age ten, and several states eliminated the minimum age entirely. Other states are considering doing this as well.

Consequently over the past ten years the rate at which children have been tried as adults has gone up 70 percent. In 1998 alone, over twenty thousand children were tried in adult courts and sent to adult prisons, and more than fifty juvenile offenders are currently on death row awaiting execution. In the Michigan correctional facility where Abraham would be housed, there are eighty-three older juveniles now serving adult sentences.

Juveniles in Adult Prisons

This trend troubles some experts because studies show that juveniles imprisoned in adult facilities do not have as great a chance of being rehabilitated as children housed in juvenile facilities, largely because of their increased contact with hardened adult criminals. As Judy Briscoe explains,

> Legitimate public concerns justify imprisoning dangerous, repeat offenders; however, research shows that housing juvenile offenders with adult felons is not the answer to decrease the rate of violent crime. Youth who get into trouble with the law need adult guidance, and suitable role models won't be found in prison.[55]

In addition, the methods for rehabilitating criminals in an adult prison are different from those used in a juvenile facility. Juvenile facilities offer inmates more structure, making it difficult for them not to participate in rehabilitative activities. In adult facilities, however, it is largely up to the inmate to seek such help. Therefore even people involved in the rights of victims rather than criminals believe it does not benefit society to house juveniles in adult prisons. For example, victims rights activist Clementine Barfield, whose sixteen-year-old son was killed in a shooting, admits that "An 11-year-old doesn't have the life experiences to know how to rehabilitate himself."[56]

But people who support the idea of imprisoning hardened young criminals in adult facilities point out that sending a child to a juvenile facility does not guarantee that child will be rehabilitated. Juveniles convicted of serious crimes are typically given psychological counseling and an education, but according to the laws in most states, most are automatically released from custody once they reach a certain age. In California, for example, a juvenile offender must be released when he or she turns twenty-five. In Arkansas, the age is twenty-one.

Automatic Release

The automatic release of young criminals upon reaching adulthood is another special juvenile right that many people believe is extremely detrimental to society. Criticism of the practice increased after August 1998, when two Arkansas boys, ages twelve and fourteen, were convicted of murdering several of their classmates in a schoolyard shooting. Because they were tried as juveniles, the murderers must be released from custody when they turn twenty-one, even though they killed one teacher and four students. They might even be released at age eighteen, because Arkansas has no facilities for juvenile criminals beyond that age.

This has upset many people, including the judge who tried the case. Under Arkansas law, Judge Ralph Wilson Jr. had no choice but to treat the boys as juveniles, and after they were found guilty he said, "Here the punishment will not fit the crime. The heinous and atrocious nature and the apparent deliberation and planned premeditation justified jail time"[57] in an adult prison as opposed to time in a juvenile rehabilitation facility.

Therefore some people advocate eliminating laws that require the release of juvenile inmates just because they have reached a predetermined age. For example, Senator Orrin Hatch of Utah was one

HENRY PAYNE. Reprinted by permission of United Feature Syndicate, Inc.

of the sponsors of a failed 1997 federal juvenile justice bill that would have prohibited the automatic release of juvenile prisoners once they become adults. In supporting the bill he said, "No one wants to have to sentence a juvenile to a lengthy prison term. But if a juvenile has committed a crime as heinous as that committed by the worst adult criminal, we must do this to protect society."[58]

Society's Well-Being

The idea that society should have the right to keep juvenile criminals in prison for many years, even into adulthood and regardless of whether they seem rehabilitated, has gained support in recent years. Under this view, an individual forfeits his or her right to freedom once convicted of a crime, and society has the right to imprison that person for as many years as lawmakers deem to be suitable punishment. This approach to the criminal justice system ignores an individual's well-being in favor of society's well-being. Pete Wilson supported this view when, as governor of California in 1997, he advocated longer juvenile sentences and added, "No longer will the welfare of the young felon be the primary concern of the juvenile justice system."[59]

Other people counter that unless the individual needs of each juvenile offender are taken into account, society will fail to reduce crime—unless society plans to lock up every young criminal for life. Many people find this prospect unacceptable. For example, a March 1998 editorial in *USA Today* states, "No person who has murdered another should be set free automatically because of his age. But neither can society turn back to the days of the late 19th century [before juvenile courts were established]. . . . With kids as young as 13 and 11, it's foolish to abandon all hope of rehabilitation."[60]

But while rehabilitation may be in the best interest of individual criminals, experts disagree on whether the effort and expense of attempting rehabilitation is in the best interest of society, since success cannot be guaranteed. People also disagree on whether a juvenile offender deserves special treatment simply by virtue of youth. The juvenile justice system was created to protect the rights of children in an era when young people were typically more naive than they are now. Some policymakers therefore suggest that it is time to reexamine that system in light of social changes that have taken place since the nineteenth century.

Chapter 4

Do Mandatory Sentencing Laws Violate Individual Rights?

IN 1995 KEVIN WEBER broke into a California restaurant and stole four chocolate cookies. The customary sentence for such a crime is three years. However, because Weber had previously been convicted of two other crimes—burglary and assault with a firearm—under a 1994 California statute called the "three-strikes law" a judge was required to sentence him to twenty-five years to life in prison. Weber's attorney asked a higher court to reconsider this sentence, but in March 1998 Judge Jean Rheinheimer decided it should stand. She said, "I just see no reason to say Mr. Weber is anything other than the three-strikes defendant the people and the Legislature had in mind when they enacted the law."[61]

Punishment Versus Protection

The three-strikes law was designed to get repeat offenders off the streets, under the reasoning that for habitual criminals, imprisonment is a way not just to punish the individual but also to protect society. Given this view, while sentencing Weber to a minimum of twenty-five years was not a fair punishment for the theft of four cookies, it was a necessary protection for society given the fact that Weber would probably continue to commit crimes in the future. In fact, upon making her decision to uphold this sentence, Judge Rheinheimer suggested that because Weber was interrupted by a burglar alarm while robbing the restaurant, he probably intended to steal more than just four cookies. California's three-strikes law mandates that anyone convicted of his or her third felony must receive that same sentence and must serve 80 percent of it, or twenty years.

Supporters of three-strikes laws, and other laws that mandate a specific sentence for all crimes of the same type, argue that such laws are a long-needed response to a crime rate that is out of control. For example, California attorney Brent Romney says, "Once a person's committed two serious or violent felonies, the emphasis should be on protecting society rather than worrying about helping the criminal. . . . Incarceration is not the best answer, but right now it's the best answer to protect society."[62]

Opponents to such laws, however, call them an overreaction to what are inarguably legitimate problems. For example, in criticizing a mandatory sentencing law that requires anyone caught with more than a pound of cocaine to serve a life sentence, Michigan state representative Barbara Dobb says, "A lot of the people [sentenced under this law] were young people who made very stupid mistakes but shouldn't have to pay for it for the rest of their lives."[63]

Equal Treatment

Arguments regarding such laws take place throughout the country, with the debate revolving around a central issue: whether society's right to protect itself from crime supercedes a defendant's right to be treated as an individual. Mandatory sentencing laws give no consideration to the unique elements of each crime. Offenses are placed in broad categories—violent or nonviolent crimes, for example—and all criminals who have committed a crime of the same category are treated in exactly the same way, regardless of individual circumstances. Prior to such laws, given two burglars who committed the same crime, one might be released from prison after serving fifteen years of a twenty-year sentence, while the other might be released after serving just one year. With mandatory sentencing laws, these kinds of disparities can no longer occur.

Therefore the appeal of mandatory sentencing laws is that in theory they are fair. All burglars serve the same amount of time in prison and, in the case of three-strikes laws, all criminals who commit a third felony are locked up for at least twenty-five years. There

Under mandatory sentencing laws, criminals who have committed similar crimes receive equal sentences.

is no confusion regarding the consequences of criminal behavior, and no one can get out of prison early just for behaving well behind bars. Jail time is determined by the type of crime a person committed.

The possibility that a criminal might serve only part of a sentence because of good prison behavior is what initially drove the movement to establish three-strikes and other mandatory sentencing laws throughout the country. California's three-strikes law, for example, was a direct result of a murder case involving a released felon, Richard Allen Davis. In 1993, Davis broke into a house where several twelve-year-old girls were having a slumber party. Threatening them with a knife, he tied up all but one, Polly Klaas, whom he carried away. Davis was apprehended over a month later, and he led police to Polly's body.

Habitual Criminals

This crime outraged the American public, not only because of Polly's brutal death but also because Davis had been sent to prison several times for violent crimes but on each occasion was released

Three-strikes laws are aimed at keeping habitual criminals, such as Richard Allen Davis (pictured), in jail.

early. Shortly before Klaas's murder, he was set free after serving only eight years of a sixteen-year sentence for kidnapping and robbery. The first time he was sent to prison, he served only one year of a fifteen-year sentence for burglary. When this information was made public, many people demanded some form of mandatory sentencing to prevent other violent criminals from being paroled after serving only a fraction of their allotted prison time. They also demanded that repeat criminals like Davis be given much longer sentences than first-time offenders.

In 1993 Washington State created the first three-strikes law, mandating long sentences for repeat offenders. Since then, twenty-four other states have enacted some form of two-strikes or three-strikes laws, mandating harsher sentences for repeat offenders. In addition, twenty-seven states and the District of Columbia now require violent offenders to serve at least 85 percent of their sentences, and thirteen states require them to serve a substantial percentage of their minimum sentences. Fourteen states have eliminated the power of parole boards to release any prisoners early, while six have eliminated their ability to release violent or felony offenders.

The benefit of keeping habitual criminals in prison is obvious. A person prone to commit violent acts will always be a danger to society unless that person is somehow rehabilitated, and such rehabilitation is far from likely in modern prisons. Studies indicate that people who have served time in prison have a high incidence of repeating criminal behavior. For example, in 1998, 41 percent of all Wisconsin parolees committed a new offense within three years of their release from prison, and 17 percent of the criminals entering prisons that year were there because of parole violations.

Considering Motivation

Three-strikes laws assure that repeat offenders, who have shown over and over again that they cannot live by the rules of society, will not be free to commit another crime. But the problem with simplifying a rule to this extent is that individual circumstances are not taken into account when determining sentences. Both three-strikes and mandatory sentencing laws give no allowances for the reasons behind a particular criminal act. Yet the essence of the justice system involves determining motivation; in judging guilt, the *why* is as important as the *what*. As James Q. Wilson of the *Washington Times* explains: "Justice does not mean applying the law without regard to circumstances. If a frightfully abused child kills his abusive father, we do not—we cannot—treat him as we would treat a Mafia hit man who might use the same weapon to kill in the same way an innocent shopkeeper." [64]

But when the courts no longer have any discretion in sentencing criminals, injustice can occur. Petty thieves like Kevin Weber can be sentenced to life in prison for stealing four cookies or, as was the case with Michael Riggs, for shoplifting a bottle of vitamins. In 1995 Riggs was convicted under California's three-strikes law after stealing vitamins because he had previously committed four nonviolent crimes and four robberies. His sentence was twenty-five years to life in prison, with no possibility of early release until he had served twenty of those years.

Riggs's attorney appealed this sentence, but in January 1999 the U.S. Supreme Court rejected the appeal. Craig Nelson, a California state deputy attorney general, was pleased with this decision. He says that given the man's history of criminal behavior, "the sentence was not cruel and unusual punishment." [65]

However, several of the Supreme Court justices did express some concerns about Riggs's punishment. They suggested that California's three-strikes law, while constitutional, needed to be reviewed by the state to make sure sentences remain fair in relation to the crime. The justices wrote that California "appears to be the only state in which a misdemeanor [minor crime] could receive such a severe sentence." [66]

Amending the Law

In fact, California Supreme Court rulings have already led to changes in California's three-strikes law because of concerns over unfairness. In 1996, it ruled that judges can decide whether the crime being tried is a felony or a misdemeanor rather than leaving that decision solely to district attorneys, as was the case with the first version of the three-strikes law. Because district attorneys are elected officials, they sometimes make decisions based on public

Third Strike Cases in California by Ethnicity and Gender as of May 31, 1999

Source: Families to Amend California's Three-Strikes.

	Female	Male	Total	Percentage
Black	26	2338	2364	44.3%
Hispanic-Mexican	6	1381	1387	26.0%
White	17	1340	1357	25.4%
Other	5	222	227	4.3%
Total	54	5281	5335	100.0%

opinion. Therefore they might decide to charge a person with a felony because it is politically expedient. But once convicted of a felony that should have been tried as a misdemeanor, under three-strikes a criminal would have to receive a stiff sentence.

For example, in March 1995 a district attorney in California decided to prosecute the theft of food as a felony. Jerry Williams had taken a slice of pizza from four children on a pier, and because he had previously been convicted of robbery and drug possession, he received twenty-five years to life in prison. However, when the state supreme court amended California's three-strikes law, it ordered every case that had already been tried under that law to be reviewed for fairness. As a result, his sentence was reduced.

In this way, the California Supreme Court decision impacted past cases. It also will impact future ones by allowing judges to determine which crimes deserve to be tried as felonies. Since three-strikes sentences are based on felony convictions rather than misdemeanors, a judge now has the power to keep someone from getting a third felony conviction, or strike.

But even after the court's ruling, critics still say that California's three-strikes law is unfair. They point out that in the state's major cities, blacks are being imprisoned for their third strike at a rate thirteen to seventeen times greater than whites. Therefore they believe that the application of the law is racist. As Vincent Schiraldi, a legal expert who has studied the law in California, says: "If one were writing a law to deliberately target blacks, one could scarcely have done it more effectively than three strikes."[67]

In fact, throughout the country most criminals sentenced under three-strikes laws are African American. One possible reason for this disparity might be that African Americans commit more crimes than whites (based on their number in the population). Opponents of mandatory sentencing argue, however, that minorities are unfairly penalized by three-strikes laws because such laws do not take into account the special circumstances of each crime. Many of the African Americans sentenced under three-strikes laws are from the lowest economic levels of society, and their crimes are related to their poverty. But under three-strikes, no allowances are made for a criminal's background. Therefore critics advocate that such laws be abolished.

Reducing Crime

Despite criticism, three-strikes laws remain popular, and the number of criminals impacted by them is growing. In California, for example, over forty thousand criminals received their second or third strike between 1994, when the law was enacted, and January 1999. During that time approximately forty-four hundred people were sentenced to twenty-five years to life. Statistics also show that during the same period, violent crime in California dropped 26.2 percent. Many people believe that the three-strikes law caused the reduction in crime.

However, some experts disagree with this opinion, arguing that California's decrease in crime must be viewed in terms of crime trends elsewhere in the nation. To this end, analysts with the Rand Corporation, a nonpartisan "think tank" that often evaluates social programs, compared California's crime rate to rates in states without a three-strikes law and determined that there was no essential difference in those rates during the same period. In other words, crime was similarly low in states with different laws.

Regardless of statistics, common sense would suggest that keeping a habitual criminal off the streets for as long as possible reduces crime, simply because if such criminals were out of prison they would be likely to victimize the public again. Nonetheless, some people believe that mandating long sentences for repeat offenders is ultimately more detrimental to society than releasing these prisoners early, in part because one result of mandatory sentencing laws is an overburdened criminal justice system.

Faced with a possible twenty-five-years-to-life sentence, few people arrested for their third strike are willing to plead guilty; instead they demand jury trials. This can seriously clog the courts. For example, in 1996, after the three-strikes law was amended, three-strikes cases in Los Angeles County accounted for 24 percent of all jury trials, even though these cases were only 3 percent of the total criminal caseload.

Moreover, three-strikes defendants must usually await their trials in jail because law enforcement officials fear they will disappear if released. As Michael P. Judge, a Los Angeles County public defender, reports, "Three-strike defendants . . . are considered high security risk and must be housed in [the high-security] part of the jail because they are considered a flight risk."[68]

To make room for these prisoners, people who have been sentenced to a year in county jail for a misdemeanor are released after only seventy days, and most people who commit misdemeanors remain out of jail while awaiting trial. In 1994 the sheriff of Los Angeles County, Sherman Block, predicted that no one who has committed a minor crime would serve any jail time if prison overcrowding continued. He says:

> The result would be that we would have a total population of individuals in our custody who are [waiting to be tried for serious felonies], which means that we will not be able

Number of U.S. State and Federal Prisoners

Year	Total Number	% Increase
1990	773,919	
1991	825,559	6.7%
1992	882,500	6.9%
1993	970,444	7.4%
1994	1,054,702	8.7%
1995	1,125,874	6.7%
1996	1,183,368	5.1%
1997	1,244,554	5.2%

Source: Bureau of Justice Statistics.

to house any individuals who were convicted of misdemeanor offenses because we have a population cap on our
system that has been placed by the federal court. . . . If people commit a criminal offense, go through the process, are
found guilty and sentenced, and then you can't impose the
sentence, . . . what you've done is made a mockery of the
system. If the system is designed to in any way deter criminal behavior, you've lost that ability.[69]

An Expensive Law

An overcrowded criminal justice system is also more expensive to
maintain, because additional personnel and facilities are needed to
handle the increase in suspects. For example, in March 1998 Los
Angeles County officials estimated that it has cost the county an
additional $200 million to arrest, prosecute, and defend criminals
under the three-strikes law. In the first year alone, the cost was $64
million. Feeding and housing extra prisoners similarly burdens tax-
payers. The state of Georgia estimates that in 1998 the average daily

Many people argue that the criminal justice system is too expensive to
maintain under the three-strikes laws.

cost to house, feed, and clothe each of its thirty-eight thousand inmates ranged from $26 at a minimum-security facility to $78 for a prisoner awaiting execution.

For this reason, Walker Dickey, special counsel to a Georgia group called Campaign for Effective Crime Policy, argues that mandatory sentencing is too expensive for the benefits it brings to society, saying: "You can't see what the cost [of three-strikes laws] will be over time, but our children and grandchildren will have a pretty big bill. . . . [Mandatory sentencing] is not worth the cost."[70]

Moreover, an August 1998 editorial in the *Christian Science Monitor* points out that the money spent on building prisons in order to accommodate three-strikes prisoners takes money away from programs designed to rehabilitate inmates, so that when they *are* released from prison—whether it is in one year or twenty—they will not return to a life of crime. The editorial lists the benefits of these programs and says, "If bulging prisons crowd out these opportunities, the real loser is society."[71]

Violent Versus Nonviolent Offenders

To reduce prison overcrowding, some people suggest that judges and parole boards should once again be allowed the discretion to shorten prison sentences, even if the criminal has committed a third felony. But this would not solve the problem that three-strikes laws were designed to address, namely, the fact that offenders imprisoned for violent crimes—like Richard Allen Davis—often revert to violence when released from prison. Therefore rather than eliminate three-strikes laws entirely, some people have suggested that they be applied only to violent offenders. As attorney John Jenswold says,

> Obviously, the assaulters, the murderers, the rapists and those who are guilty of violence should be [serving long prison sentences]. But do we have to build these multimillion-dollar prisons and house people at something like $40,000 a year apiece to protect the public when the crimes they commit are non-violent?[72]

In fact, some states do limit their three-strikes laws to violent offenders, and this practice has reduced the number of criminals who fall under such laws. For example, Washington State has always limited its three-strikes law to violent offenders, and it has sentenced only 150 people under that law since 1993. A group called Families to Amend Three Strikes wants California to limit its three-strikes law as well. The group particularly wants to exclude people convicted of drug use from being subjected to mandatory sentencing. One of the leaders of the group, Sue Reams, says, "We don't put all the alcoholics in jail, so should we put all the drug offenders in jail for life?"[73]

Limiting three-strikes and mandatory sentencing laws to violent offenders would reduce the number of drug dealers serving long sentences under these laws. However, since those convicted of three drug offenses have demonstrated a tendency to repeat their crimes, sending them back out onto the streets will certainly not help America's drug problem. Moreover, if violence is the primary criterion for long sentences, the original goal of getting repeat offenders off the streets is weakened. The question is not only whether nonviolent criminals should be sentenced in the same way as violent ones, but also whether society is best served by three-strikes and mandatory sentencing laws.

Chapter 5

Is the Death Penalty Necessary to Protect Society?

IN FEBRUARY 1998, KARLA FAYE TUCKER became the first woman executed in Texas since the Civil War. Her death by lethal injection caused an enormous controversy, not only because of her gender but because she publicly and convincingly repented her crime.

Tucker was sentenced to death for breaking into a house and murdering two people with a pickax in 1983. At the time, she was angry because one of the victims had recently spilled motor oil on her carpet, and shortly after the incident, she stated that she had enjoyed killing. During her trial Tucker excused her behavior by saying that she had been under the influence of drugs at the time of the attack.

But over the fourteen years she spent in prison awaiting execution, her attitudes and outlook on life—as well as on the crime she committed—changed. She became a born-again Christian, and because of her religious beliefs she apologized for her actions, expressed remorse, and renounced all attempts to overturn her conviction. In addition, she married the prison chaplain and became a preacher herself.

Tucker's transformation from remorseless killer to repentant model prisoner inspired a public campaign to have her death sentence commuted to life in prison. Those who sought clemency for Tucker based their case on the view that a criminal—even one who has committed the terrible crime of murder—can be rehabilitated. Under this view, an individual who demonstrates sincere remorse

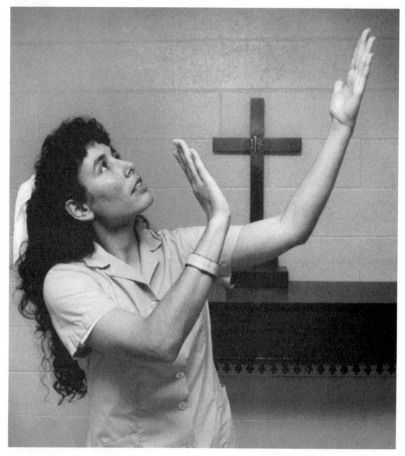

Convicted killer Karla Faye Tucker won much public sympathy but did not escape execution.

for past deeds and who can show that he or she no longer represents a danger to society, deserves forgiveness, even if that means living out one's days in prison rather than being put to death. Opponents of the death penalty for Tucker, as well as for others on death row, believe that individuals should have a higher priority than society's desire to exact punishment or revenge.

Despite a groundswell of support for Tucker, Texas officials refused to grant her clemency, and in the final hours before her death, Governor George W. Bush refused to stay her execution. Of his decision Bush said, "My attitude is you have the death penalty or you don't. If you have the death penalty, it must be administered fairly and justly based on the facts of the crime."[74]

Bush had concluded that a convicted murderer's degree of repentance or spirituality should not be the criteria for applying the death penalty. Richard Thorton, the husband of one of the people murdered by Tucker, agrees with this concept. He says: "People need to understand that Karla Faye Tucker murdered two people in cold blood. She was and is a horrible person. If she has found religion, then God bless her. But she was found guilty, she was sentenced to death. She needs to die."[75]

Should Repentance Matter?

The issue of whether repentant murderers should be executed is controversial. In fact, it is just one of many controversies swirling around the death penalty in the United States. Some Americans

Protesters rally in hopes of halting the execution of Karla Faye Tucker.

believe that the death penalty defiles the American way of life by placing the needs of the majority above the needs of the individual. Others see the death penalty as a necessary evil in a society that must be protected from violence.

Those who hold the latter view believe that public safety demands clear and severe consequences for those who violate the law. They further believe that society is always better off executing murderers, regardless of their mental state, because of the validation the execution gives to victims and the message it sends to others who might murder. For example, reporter Sandy Banks argues that Tucker's victims had to be considered in deciding her fate, suggesting that those victims deserved to have their deaths avenged:

> I find it hard to feel sorry for [Tucker], to accept her execution as unjust. She had, at least, 14 years to prepare to die—time to repent, to accept the Lord, to be "born again" and prepare her heart for the afterlife she believed awaited her. That's more than [her victims] got. More than you or I will probably get. And it's all the mercy she deserved.[76]

Tony Snow, a reporter for the *Detroit News*, says that Tucker had to die in order to prevent other death-row prisoners from feigning rehabilitation. He explains:

> The crusade [to pardon Tucker] forced Texas authorities to confront the question: Do you carve out exceptions to the law when a murderer, through God's grace, repents? The parole board eventually replied: Nope. The law's the law. From a legal standpoint, the board was right. You can't suspend the statutes every time somebody . . . [becomes religious]. If you did, our prisons quickly would be awash in penitent tears, and every homicidal maniac would be weeping and reciting scriptures.[77]

Snow implies that the main motivation behind the decision to execute Tucker was fairness. Tucker should not have been excused for her crime simply because of her religion; otherwise atheists would be at a disadvantage in the American legal system. Most people would agree that American society has the right to maintain law and order, but only if punishments are applied fairly. When society exacts unequal justice, death-penalty opponents say, it violates the individual rights on which the nation was built.

Unfair Applications

But some studies indicate that the death penalty is not being enforced fairly. Statistically, some groups receive the death penalty more than others. For example, of the thirty-eight states that currently have the death penalty, not all implement it to the same degree. A person living in a southern state is far more likely to be executed than one in the Northeast. In 1997, of the fifty-three inmates executed nationwide, forty-six were in southern prisons, but only four in the Midwest, three in the West, and none in the Northeast.

Another disparity exists in regard to gender. Between 1976 and 1997, the only woman executed anywhere in the United States was Velma Barfield, a North Carolina grandmother who poisoned her fiancé. In addition, although one out of every eight Americans arrested for murder is a woman, only one out of seventy sentenced

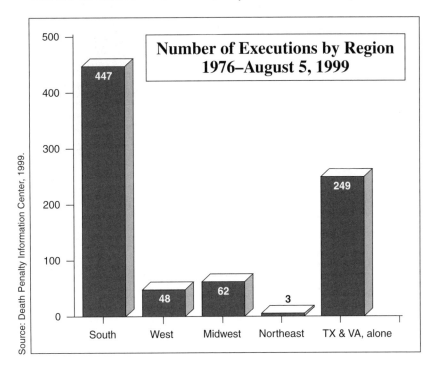

Number of Executions by Region
1976–August 5, 1999

Source: Death Penalty Information Center, 1999.

to death is a woman, and only 2 percent of women who receive the death penalty are actually executed.

Therefore when Tucker was awaiting death, many people expressed the sentiment that her case would not have attracted attention had she been a man, regardless of her spiritual beliefs. For example, Victor Streib, a law professor at Ohio Northern University, has studied the justice system and determined that women receive special treatment not only after receiving the death penalty but also before. He explains, "Prosecutors are more reluctant to charge women with capital murder, and juries more easily believe that women are under emotional distress while committing a crime."[78]

However, Streib suggests that such discrepancies in the treatment of male and female criminals are due more to the nature of women's crimes than to gender. He explains: "[I]n our society we consider it worse, or more likely to be punished, if you've killed a stranger, and women, when they kill, are much more likely to kill a family member [who has abused them]."[79]

Statistics also indicate that race and economic class influence the implementation of the death penalty. An African American is far more likely to be sentenced to death than a white, particularly if the victim is white. In 1994, for example, blacks who killed whites received the death penalty twenty-two times more often than blacks who killed blacks, and over seven times more often than whites who killed blacks. Moreover, wealthy defendants typically avoid the death penalty because they can afford to hire lawyers skilled at helping clients accused of capital crimes.

Executing Innocents

The U.S. Supreme Court has long been concerned about such inequities. From 1972 to 1976, the Court placed a moratorium on the death penalty because it was being applied in a seemingly arbitrary fashion. State laws were rewritten to solve this problem, and the penalty was reinstated. However, the statistics suggest that the problem still exists. Therefore in 1994 Supreme Court justice Harry A. Blackmun announced that although he had supported the death penalty for twenty-five years, he would no longer do so. He said that the justice system, or what he called "the machinery of death," had

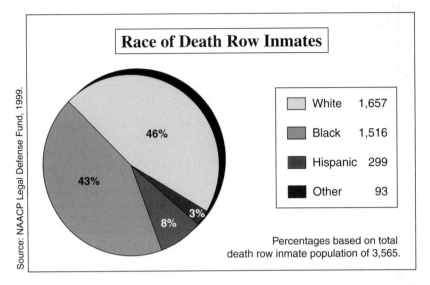

Race of Death Row Inmates

Source: NAACP Legal Defense Fund, 1999.

46%

43%

8%   3%

	White	1,657
	Black	1,516
	Hispanic	299
	Other	93

Percentages based on total
death row inmate population of 3,565.

become too "fraught with arbitrariness, discrimination, caprice and mistake"[80] to be supportable.

In using the word "mistake," Justice Blackmun referred to the possibility that an innocent person might be executed. It is inevitable that this will occur because, as U.S. Supreme Court justice Thurgood Marshall once wrote: "No matter how careful the courts are, the possibility of perjured testimony, mistaken honest testimony, and human error remain all too real. We have no way of judging how many innocent persons have been executed, but we can be certain that there were some."[81]

Since the 1970s, more than seventy people have been released from death row because they were wrongfully convicted or received an unfair trial. Many of these people were poor and black. In describing the typical circumstances surrounding a false conviction, reporter Arlene Levinson notes the connection between a prisoner's background and a false conviction:

> No physical evidence, no eyewitness, a jail-house snitch, claims of a confession but no record of one, investigators using weak or suspect "science": these are hallmarks of wrongful convictions. . . . Individuals caught in this deadly net also are apt to be from society's fringes: poor, minority and criminal. Typically, their lawyers do a poor job. Reversals

usually come from new evidence pointing to the real killer, a recanting witness, and, less often, DNA testing.[82]

The risk that an innocent person might be executed has led to much of the opposition to the death penalty. In the view of opponents to the death penalty, society has the right to maintain order and punish wrongdoers, but its needs should not outweigh an individual's right to fair treatment and a just disposition of a criminal case—especially when that case could end in an execution.

Retribution for Horrible Acts

Justice is also a concern for death penalty supporters. The thought of executing an innocent man or woman is repulsive no matter what one's views of the death penalty. Rather than abandon the death penalty altogether, though, supporters say that the justice system must redouble its efforts to ensure fairness and justice. To do away with capital punishment devalues the life of the individual who was killed and eliminates a critical tool for maintaining order.

Robert Bork, a former federal judge and a fellow of the conservative American Enterprise Institute in Washington, D.C., says that while the idea that an innocent person might be executed is disturbing, it should not convince the American public that the death penalty is unnecessary to society. He argues that the threat of execution deters people from committing serious crimes. Therefore abolishing the death penalty would mean that society has condemned innocent people rather than murderers to death, because without the fear of capital punishment there will be nothing to restrain criminals from committing violent acts.

Moreover, Bork suggests that it is psychologically important for society to see criminals punished. He sees punishment not only as a way to enforce order but also as a way to release anger and make a firm statement about society's values. Bork explains: "[Putting a criminal to death] is one way of vindicating the community, relieving the community's need to express itself, for retribution, in particular for horrible acts."[83]

Columnist Eric Pooley agrees that society needs to implement the death penalty in order to express its aversion to murder, but he emphasizes this implementation should come from a position of retribution rather than revenge. The former is a rational act based on feelings of moral duty, while the latter is a passionate, instinctive response to emotional pain, a desire to make people pay for their crimes. Pooley explains: "There's a distinction to be made between revenge—a hot, deeply personal desire to hurt the malefactor—and retribution—a statelier and more carefully considered decision to uphold the values of society."[84] He believes that this desire for retribution is an acceptable reason for upholding the death penalty. As philosopher Walter Berns writes:

> Capital punishment serves to remind us of the majesty of the moral order that is embodied in our law and of the terrible consequences of its breach. . . . The criminal law must be made awful, by which I mean awe-inspiring, or commanding "profound respect or reverential fear." It must remind us of the moral order by which alone we can live as human beings.[85]

Pooley sees the death penalty as the only moral choice for a society charged with protecting its citizens. David Gelernter, a professor of computer science at Yale who was seriously injured in a

Death Penalty by State

States with death penalty:

ALABAMA	KENTUCKY	OHIO
ARIZONA	LOUISIANA	OKLAHOMA
ARKANSAS	MARYLAND	OREGON
CALIFORNIA	MISSISSIPPI	PENNSYLVANIA
COLORADO	MISSOURI	SOUTH CAROLINA
CONNECTICUT*	MONTANA	SOUTH DAKOTA*
DELAWARE	NEBRASKA	TENNESSEE
FLORIDA	NEVADA	TEXAS
GEORGIA	NEW HAMPSHIRE*	UTAH
IDAHO	NEW JERSEY*	VIRGINIA
ILLINOIS	NEW MEXICO*	WASHINGTON
INDIANA	NEW YORK*	WYOMING
KANSAS*	NORTH CAROLINA	

*Retains death penalty but has not implemented it in at least 10 years.

States without death penalty:

ALASKA	MASSACHUSETTS	RHODE ISLAND
HAWAII	MICHIGAN	VERMONT
IOWA	MINNESOTA	WEST VIRGINIA
MAINE	NORTH DAKOTA	WISCONSIN
		– plus DISTRICT OF COLUMBIA

Source: Death Penalty Information Center, 1999.

letter-bomb attack in June 1993, supports this position. Gelernter believes that "a deliberate murderer embodies evil so terrible that it defiles the community."[86] He therefore argues that society needs the death penalty because the act restores order and proclaims that murder will not be tolerated.

Moreover, because putting someone to death is a dramatic and final act, Gelernter says that it is essential that life imprisonment not be offered as an alternative for those who commit murder. In Gelernter's opinion, nothing less than the death penalty will serve society. He explains:

Among possible responses, the death penalty is uniquely powerful because it is permanent and can never be retracted or overturned. An execution forces the community to assume forever the burden of moral certainty; it is a form of absolute speech that allows no waffling or equivocation. Deliberate murder, the community announces, is absolutely evil and absolutely intolerable, period.[87]

In other words, society has not only the right to execute but also the obligation to do so. The needs of the individual criminal are far less important than the needs of the greater community. Or, as Gelernter says, "If we favor executing murderers it is not because we want to but because, however much we do not want to, we consider ourselves obliged to."[88]

Debasing Society and Human Beings

However, some people believe that killing human beings is wrong, no matter what the reason, and that participating in murder weakens the moral and social fabric of the country. They point out that a society is actually made up of individuals, and argue that each of those individuals must be valued in order to maintain the integrity of the community. In other words, individual needs and societal needs are essentially the same.

An October 17, 1993, editorial in the *Wisconsin State Journal* expresses this view when it says, "The state—which ought to act to protect life—debases itself when it acts to take away life. It cheapens

Many death penalty opponents believe that every individual in a society has worth and should be valued.

the value of life in society and contributes to the notion that violence is a solution to the world's problems."[89] David Gelernter's critics also use moral arguments to attack his position that society needs to kill murderers. For example, in response to one of Gelernter's articles, Dane M. Johnston writes: "Killing is killing. Execution is a form of deliberate murder and subject to the same declarations of evil and intolerance."[90]

Many people outside of America share this view. For example, Marie-Claire Perrault of Canada, where no one has been put to death since 1962, says: "A society that kills its own citizens is a sick, sad society."[91] Canada officially abolished the death penalty in 1988, and many other nations have done this as well. The United Nations does not support execution, nor does the Council of Europe or the International Court of Justice, and many countries refuse to extradite criminals to the United States specifically because the death penalty exists here. Stefanie Grant, an expert on international law, explains that the international community condemns the death penalty "based on the human rights principles of the right to life and the right to be protected from cruel, inhuman, and degrading punishment contained in the Universal Declaration of Human Rights."[92]

In discussing this movement, Grant quotes the decision of the South African Constitution Court that

> Retribution cannot be accorded the same weight under our Constitution as the rights to life and dignity. . . . It has not been shown that the death sentence would be materially more effective to deter or prevent murder. . . . Taking these factors into account, as well as the elements of arbitrariness and the possibility of error . . . the clear and convincing case that is required to justify the death sentence . . . has not been made out.[93]

Moreover, many people hold the conviction that killing is morally wrong, even when it is done with the sanction of the state, and even when the person murdered is evil. Grant quotes a document of the UN Security Council as saying, "We do not believe that following the principle of 'an eye for an eye' [killing a killer] is the path to establishing a civilized society, no matter how horrendous the crimes the individuals concerned may have committed."[94]

Reprinted by permission of Harley Schwadron.

"MAYBE THIS WILL TEACH YOU THAT IT'S MORALLY WRONG TO KILL PEOPLE!"

Similarly, Bo Lozoff of the Human Kindness Foundation suggests that it is wrong to devalue a human life, no matter what the reason:

> What do murderers deserve? The same thing all of society deserves: to be treated as human beings with complex potential for good and evil acts; to be held accountable for their behavior without being prevented from changing for the better; to be given some opportunity to help the common good even from a prison cell.[95]

Lozoff works with prison inmates who give talks to other criminals, telling them how to improve their lives and avoid committing more serious crimes after their release. He believes that such acts of atonement help society far more than executions do. Nonetheless, approximately 75 percent of the American public currently approves of the death penalty, and there is no sign of that support weakening. Most Americans firmly believe that society's right to execute its most violent criminals outweighs an individual's right to life.

Conclusion ■

Crime and Punishment

IT IS NOT ALWAYS possible to determine the best way to solve a crime-related problem, if in fact it can be solved at all. Experts disagree on many issues, including whether the death penalty and mandatory sentencing laws deter crime, whether children should be tried as adults, whether society should restrict citizens' access to guns, and whether police need to be more closely regulated. In all of these situations, some people advocate strengthening the position of the individual and some advocate strengthening the position of society, so that one or the other has more rights and more power to use them.

The nature of the criminal justice system is also in dispute. Some people believe that its main purpose is to protect every individual's right to fair and impartial justice, while others believe that its main priority is to enforce society's right to maintain order and exact punishment. The criminal justice system is charged with both of these duties, but they are difficult

Determining whether a young person should be tried as an adult is one of many crime-related issues debated today.

80

to balance because at times society and the individual appear to have competing interests. For example, stealing money from a store might benefit a particular individual, but if everyone were allowed to steal money without consequence, then social order would be destroyed.

However, in actuality the interests of the individual and the interests of society are one and the same. Even a thief wants to be protected from robbery. When social order is maintained, individuals are rewarded with peace and security. Conversely, when individual needs are met, society is rewarded with happier and more productive citizens. To lose sight of the individuals who make up society is to lose sight of the essence that creates a society in the first place.

Notes

Introduction: The Rights of Individuals Versus the Rights of Society

1. Diane Whiteley, "The Victim and the Justification of Punishment," *Criminal Justice Ethics*, June 22, 1998, p. 42.
2. James Q. Wilson and Susanne Washburn, "A Rhythm to the Madness," *Time*, August 23, 1993, p. 31.
3. Quoted in Harold J. Rothwax, *Guilty: The Collapse of Criminal Justice*. New York: Warner Books, 1997, p. 40.
4. Rothwax, *Guilty*, p. 41.
5. Rothwax, *Guilty*, p. 40.
6. Rothwax, *Guilty*, p. 22.

Chapter 1: Should the Powers of Police Be Diminished?

7. Quoted in Barbara Dority, "More Power, Less Responsibility," *Humanist*, September 19, 1998, p. 3.
8. Quoted in Dority, "More Power, Less Responsibility," p. 3.
9. Sam Newlund, "High-Speed Police Chases Are a Risky Business That We'd Do Better to Ban," *Minneapolis Star Tribune*, May 12, 1996, p. 29A.
10. Dority, "More Power, Less Responsibility," p. 3.
11. Quoted in Rick Van Sant, "Cost of Police Chases Too High," *Denver Rocky Mountain News*, August 30, 1998, p. 3A.
12. Richard Moran and Bob Edwards, "High-Speed Chases," *Morning Edition*, National Public Radio, October 14, 1997.
13. Paul D. Linnee, "Limit Police Pursuit and Bad Guys Will Escape," *Minneapolis Star Tribune*, December 19, 1998, p. 33A.

14. Linnee, "Limit Police Pursuit and Bad Guys Will Escape," p. 33A.
15. Linnee, "Limit Police Pursuit and Bad Guys Will Escape," p. 33A.
16. Quoted in Dority, "More Power, Less Responsibility," p. 3.
17. Quoted in Herbert A. Sample, "Police Chase Ends in High Court," *Denver Rocky Mountain News*, December 8, 1997, p. 3A.
18. Newlund, "High-Speed Police Chases Are a Risky Business That We'd Do Better to Ban," p. 29A.
19. Newlund, "High-Speed Police Chases Are a Risky Business That We'd Do Better to Ban," p. 29A.
20. Quoted in Ted Koppel, "The Blue Wall," part 1, *ABC Nightline*, August 21, 1997.
21. Quoted in William Raspberry, "We Too Easily Overlook Some Violations," *Dallas Morning News,* October 13, 1998, p. 15A.
22. Samuel D. Faulkner and Larry P. Danaher, "Controlling Subjects: Realistic Training vs. Magic Bullets," *FBI Law Enforcement Bulletin*, February 1, 1997, p. 21.
23. Faulkner and Danaher, "Controlling Subjects," p. 26.
24. Georgette Bennett, *Crime Warps: The Future of Crime in America*. New York: Anchor Books, 1989, p. 310.
25. Anthony J. Pinizzotto, Edward F. Davis, and Charles E. Miller III, "In the Line of Fire: Learning from Assaults on Law Enforcement Officers," *FBI Law Enforcement Bulletin*, February 1, 1998, p. 19.
26. Quoted in Warren Richey, "High Court Expands Police Power to Search," *Christian Science Monitor*, April 7, 1999.
27. Ray Suarez, "Victims' Rights," *Talk of the Nation*, National Public Radio, July 7, 1998.

Chapter 2: Should Society Restrict Access to Guns?

28. Washington Transcript Service, "U.S. Representative Charles Schumer (D-NY) Holds News Conference on Gun Control," May 22, 1998.
29. Sylvia Kinyoun, "Wise Founders," letter to the editor, *Ventura County Star*, July 11, 1999.

30. Ray Suarez, "Kids and Gun Violence," *Talk of the Nation*, National Public Radio, March 31, 1998.

31. Quoted in Washington Transcript Service, "U.S. Senator Barbara Boxer (D-CA) Holds News Conference to Discuss Brady Law Implementation," November 30, 1998.

32. Jacob Sullum, "Weapon Assault: The Advantage of Weak Arguments," *Reason*, July 1, 1994, p. 5.

33. Sullum, "Weapon Assault," p. 5.

34. Josh Sugarman, "Reverse Fire: The Brady Bill Won't Break the Sick Hold Guns Have on America. It's Time for Tougher Measures," *Mother Jones*, January 1, 1994, p. 36.

35. Sugarman, "Reverse Fire," p. 36.

36. Inter Press News Service English Newswire, "Jamaica: Government Moves to Halt Bloody Crime Wave," July 15, 1999.

37. Quoted in Suarez, "Kids and Gun Violence."

38. Scott Burger, "Controlling Criminals, Not Guns, Prevents Trouble," *Rocky Mountain Collegian/University Wire*, October 1, 1998.

39. Sean Hannity and Alan Colmes, "Los Angeles Shootings," *Hannity and Colmes*, Fox News Network, August 11, 1999.

40. Paul Braun, "Freedom at Risk," letter to the editor, *Ventura County Star*, July 11, 1999.

41. Quoted in Washington Transcript Service, "U.S. Representative Charles Schumer (D-NY) Holds News Conference on Gun Control."

42. Quoted in Hannity and Colmes, "Los Angeles Shootings."

43. Quoted in Ira J. Hadnot, "John Lott Jr.: Interview," *Dallas Morning News*, May 31, 1998, p. 1J.

44. Bob Barr, "Gun Laws Don't Work," a sidebar within Patricia V. Rivera's article "Gun Laws Don't Work," *USA Today*, December 19, 1995.

45. Quoted in Suarez, "Kids and Gun Violence."

Chapter 3: Should Children Who Murder Be Treated as Adults?

46. Charlie Weaver, "Violent Youth Must Get Clear Message: You'll Be Held Accountable," *Minneapolis Star Tribune*, February 5, 1998, p. 22A.

47. Judy Briscoe, "Breaking the Cycle of Violence: A Rational Approach to At-Risk Youth," *Federal Probation*, September 1, 1997.

48. Quoted in Suarez, "Jonesboro Convictions," *Talk of the Nation*, National Public Radio, August 12, 1998.

49. Linda Bernard, "Michigan Speaks with a Forked Tongue on Youth Issues," *Michigan Chronicle*, June 16, 1998, p. 7A.

50. Quoted in Tom Jarriel, Hugh Downs, and Barbara Walters, "He's Only a Child," *ABC 20/20*, February 13, 1998.

51. John Cloud, with reporting by Harriet Barovick, Cathy Booth, and Sylvester Monroe, "Crime: For They Know Not What They Do?" *Time,* August 24, 1998, p. 65.

52. Quoted in Cloud and others, "Crime," pp. 65–66.

53. Quoted in Jarriel, Downs, and Walters, "He's Only a Child."

54. Quoted in Jarriel, Downs, and Walters, "He's Only a Child."

55. Briscoe, "Breaking the Cycle of Violence."

56. Quoted in Jarriel, Downs, and Walters, "He's Only a Child."

57. Quoted in Briscoe, "Breaking the Cycle of Violence."

58. Quoted in Deborah Mathis and Chris Collins, "Jonesboro Attack Leaves Many Questions on Children, Justice," Gannett News Service, April 4, 1998, p. ARC.

59. Carl Ingram, "Wilson Proposes Overhaul of Juvenile Justice System," *Los Angeles Times*, April 10, 1997, p. A3.

60. *USA Today,* "Adult Time for Adult Crime? 'Blending' Is a Better Way," March 30, 1998, p. 14A.

Chapter 4: Do Mandatory Sentencing Laws Violate Individual Rights?

61. Quoted in Associated Press Online, "Judge: Cookie Thief Must Serve 'Three-Strikes' Sentence," March 15, 1998.

62. Quoted in Lisa Richardson, "Activists Seek to Limit Three-Strikes Law Sentencing," *Los Angeles Times*, August 17, 1998, p. A3.

63. Quoted in John Cloud, with reporting by Andrew Goldstein, Elaine Rivera, Viveca Novak, Elaine Shannon, and Kermit Pat, "Law: A Get-Tough Policy That Failed," *Time,* February 1, 1999, p. 48.

64. James Q. Wilson, "Restoring Sanity to a Criminal Justice System Gone Astray," *Washington Times*, April 12, 1998, p. 28.

65. Quoted in Associated Press, "High Court Upholds California's 3-Strikes Law," *Dallas Morning News*, January 20, 1999, p. 3A.

66. Quoted in Associated Press, "High Court Upholds California's 3-Strikes Law."

67. Quoted in Dave Zweifel, "After 2 Years, No Justice in '3 Strikes,'" *Madison (WI) Capital Times*, March 13, 1996, p. 11A.

68. Quoted in Emanuel Parker, "'3 Strikes Bad, Costly, Ineffective': County Public Defender," *Los Angeles Sentinel*, April 26, 1995.

69. Quoted in Linda Wertheimer, "Three Strikes Law Packs Jails in California," *All Things Considered*, National Public Radio, September 30, 1994.

70. Quoted in Rhonda Cook, "Three Strikes, You're Broke," *Atlanta Constitution*, November 13, 1998.

71. *Christian Science Monitor*, "Bulging Prisons: Editorials," August 21, 1998, p. 16.

72. John Jenswold, "Big Prisons Won't End Crime," *Madison (WI) Capital Times*, May 21, 1998, p. 14A.

73. Quoted in Richardson, "Activists Seek to Limit Three-Strikes Law Sentencing."

Chapter 5: Is the Death Penalty Necessary to Protect Society?

74. Quoted in Lee Hancock, "Death Sentence Debate Centers on Gender," *Dallas Morning News*, January 25, 1998, p. 1A.

75. Quoted in Sandy Banks, "Life as We Live It: Did Tucker Really Deserve Our Pity?" *Los Angeles Times*, February 6, 1998, p. E1.

76. Banks, "Life as We Live It," p. E1.

77. Tony Snow, "Capital Punishment: Most Arguments Against It Don't Hold Up," *Dallas Morning News*, February 5, 1998, p. 23A.

78. Quoted in Scott Baldauf, "Death Row Has Its Own Gender Gap," *Christian Science Monitor*, January 23, 1998, p. 1.

79. Quoted in Edward Lifson, "Governor Stops Woman's Death on Day of Execution," *All Things Considered*, National Public Radio, January 16, 1996.

80. Richard Cohen, "Poverty Can Be Fatal Mistake," *St. Louis Post-Dispatch*, March 17, 1994, p. 7B.
81. Quoted in Eric Pooley et al., "Crime and Punishment: Death or Life? McVeigh Could Be the Best Argument for Executions, but His Case Highlights the Problems That Arise When Death Sentences Are Churned Out in Huge Numbers," *Time,* June 16, 1997, p. 31.
82. Arlene Levinson, "Wrongly Accused Find Themselves at Death's Door," (Vancouver, WA) *Columbian,* November 11, 1998.
83. Quoted in Levinson, "Wrongly Accused Find Themselves at Death's Door."
84. Pooley, "Crime and Punishment," p. 31.
85. Quoted in Pooley, "Crime and Punishment," p. 31.
86. David Gelernter, "What Do Murderers Deserve?" *Commentary*, April 1, 1998, p. 21.
87. Gelernter, "What Do Murderers Deserve?" p. 21.
88. Gelernter, "What Do Murderers Deserve?" p. 21.
89. *Wisconsin State Journal*, "Capital Punishment: It's the Wrong Answer," October 17, 1993, p. 10A.
90. Dane M. Johnston, "The Unforgiven," letter to the editor, *Utne Reader*, June 1999, pp. 7–8.
91. Marie-Claire Perrault, "The Unforgiven," letter to the editor, *Utne Reader*, June 1999, p. 7.
92. Stefanie Grant, "A Dialogue of the Deaf? New International Attitudes and the Death Penalty in America," *Criminal Justice Ethics*, June 22, 1998, p. 19.
93. Grant, "A Dialogue of the Deaf?" p. 19.
94. Grant, "A Dialogue of the Deaf?" p. 19.
95. Bo Lozoff, "The Unforgiven," letter to the editor, *Utne Reader*, June 1999, p. 7.

ORGANIZATIONS TO CONTACT

American Civil Liberties Union (ACLU)
125 Broad St., 18th Fl.
New York, NY 10004-2400
(212) 549-2500
e-mail: aclu@aclu.org • website: www.aclu.org

The ACLU is a national organization that works to defend Americans' civil rights as guaranteed by the U.S. Constitution. It opposes curfew laws for juveniles and others and seeks to protect the public-assembly rights of gang members or people associated with gangs. Among the ACLU's numerous publications are the handbook *The Rights of Prisoners: A Comprehensive Guide to the Legal Rights of Prisoners Under Current Law*, and the briefing paper "Crime and Civil Liberties."

Campaign for an Effective Crime Policy
918 F St. NW, Suite 505
Washington, DC 20004
(202) 628-1903 • fax: (202) 628-1091
e-mail: staff@crimepolicy.org • website: www.crimepolicy.org

Launched in 1992 by a group of criminal justice leaders, the nonpartisan Campaign for an Effective Crime Policy advocates alternative sentencing policies. It also works to educate the public about the relative effectiveness of various strategies for improving public safety. The campaign has published a series of reports on issues in criminal justice, including "'Three Strikes' Laws: Five Years Later."

Cato Institute
1000 Massachusetts Ave. NW
Washington, DC 20001-5403
(202) 842-0200 • fax: (202) 842-3490
e-mail: cato@cato.org • website: www.cato.org

The institute is a libertarian public policy research foundation dedicated to limiting the role of government and protecting individual liberties. It opposes gun control measures and the death penalty and supports concealed-carry laws. The institute evaluates government policies and offers reform proposals in its publication *Policy Analysis.* Topics include "Crime, Police, and Root Causes" and "Prison Blues: How America's Foolish Sentencing Policies Endanger Public Safety." In addition, the institute publishes the quarterly magazine *Regulation*, the bimonthly *Cato Policy Report*, and numerous books.

Coalition to Stop Gun Violence (CSGV)
1000 16th St. NW, Suite 603
Washington, DC 20036-5705
(202) 530-0340
e-mail: noguns@aol.com • website: www.gunfree.org

Formerly the National Coalition to Ban Handguns, the coalition lobbies at the local, state, and federal levels to ban the sale of handguns and assault weapons to individuals. It also litigates cases against firearms makers. Its publications include various informational sheets on gun violence and the *Stop Gun Violence Newsletter* and the *Firearms Litigation Reporter.*

Families Against Mandatory Minimums (FAMM)
1612 K St. NW, Suite 1400
Washington, DC 20006
(202) 822-6700 • fax: (202) 822-6704
e-mail: famm@famm.org • website: www.famm.org

FAMM is an educational organization that works to repeal mandatory minimum sentences. It provides legislators, the public, and the media with information on and analyses of minimum-sentencing laws. FAMM publishes the quarterly newsletter *FAMM-gram.*

The Heritage Foundation
214 Massachusetts Ave. NE
Washington, DC 20002-4999
(202) 546-4400 • (800) 544-4843 • fax: (202) 544-6979
e-mail: pubs@heritage.org • website: www.heritage.org

The Heritage Foundation is a conservative public policy research institute. It is a proponent of limited government and advocates tougher sentencing and the construction of more prisons. The foundation publishes articles on a variety of public policy issues in its Backgrounder series and in its quarterly journal *Policy Review.*

The John Howard Society of Canada
771 Montreal St.
Kingston, ON K7K 3J6 CANADA
(613) 542-7547 • fax: (613) 542-6824
e-mail: national@johnhoward.ca
website: www.johnhoward.ca

The John Howard Society of Canada advocates reform of the criminal justice system and monitors governmental policy to ensure fair and compassionate treatment of prisoners. It views imprisonment as a last-resort option. The organization provides education to the community, supports services to at-risk youth, and rehabilitation programs to former inmates. Its publications include the booklet *Literacy and the Courts: Protecting the Right to Understand.*

National Center on Institutions and Alternatives (NCIA)
3125 Mt. Vernon Ave.
Alexandria, VA 22305
(703) 684-0373 • fax: (703) 684-6037
e-mail: ncia@igc.apc.org • website: www.ncianet.org/ncia

NCIA works to reduce the number of people institutionalized in prisons and mental hospitals. It favors the least restrictive forms of detention for juvenile murderers, and it opposes sentencing juveniles as adults and executing juvenile murderers. NCIA publishes the book *Juvenile Decarceration: The Politics of Correctional Reform*, and the booklet *Scared Straight: Second Look.*

National Crime Prevention Council (NCPC)
1700 K St. NW, 2nd Fl.
Washington, DC 20006-3817
(202) 261-4111 • fax: (202) 296-1356
e-mail: webmaster@ncpc.org • website: www.ncpc.org

The NCPC provides training and technical assistance to groups and individuals interested in crime prevention. It advocates job training and recreation programs as means to reduce youth crime and violence. The council, which sponsors the Take a Bite Out of Crime campaign, publishes the book *Preventing Violence: Program Ideas and Examples,* the booklet *How Communities Can Bring Up Youth Free from Fear and Violence,* and the newsletter *Catalyst,* which is published ten times a year.

National Institute of Justice (NIJ)
National Criminal Justice Reference Service (NCJRS)
Box 6000
Rockville, MD 20849
(301) 519-5500 • (800) 851-3420
e-mail: askncjrs@ncjrs.org • website: www.ncjrs.org

A component of the Office of Justice Programs of the U.S. Department of Justice, the NIJ supports research on crime, criminal behavior, and crime prevention. The National Criminal Justice Reference Service acts as a clearinghouse that provides information and research about criminal justice. Its publications include the research briefs *Crime in the Schools: A Problem-Solving Approach* and *Violence Among Middle School and High School Students: Analysis and Implications for Prevention.*

National Rifle Association of America (NRA)
11250 Waples Mill Rd.
Fairfax, VA 22030
(703) 267-1000 • fax: (703) 267-3989
website: www.nra.org

The NRA, with nearly 3 million members, is America's largest organization of gun owners. It is the primary lobbying group for those who oppose gun control laws. The NRA believes that such laws violate the U.S. Constitution and do nothing to reduce crime. In addition to its monthly magazines *American Rifleman, American Hunter*, and *Incites*, the NRA publishes numerous books, bibliographies, reports, and pamphlets on gun ownership, gun safety, and gun control.

Violence Policy Center (VPC)
2000 P St. NW, Suite 200
Washington, DC 20036
(202) 822-8200 • fax: (202) 822-8205
e-mail: comment@vpc.org • website: www.vpc.org

The center is an educational foundation that conducts research on firearms violence. It works to educate the public concerning the dangers of guns and supports gun-control measures. The center's publications include the report "Cease Fire: A Comprehensive Strategy to Reduce Firearms Violence" and the books *NRA: Money, Firepower, and Fear* and *Assault Weapons and Accessories in America*.

FOR FURTHER READING

Kelly C. Anderson, *Police Brutality*. San Diego, CA: Lucent Books, 1995. This book for young people provides an overview on the issue of police brutality.

Ian Gray and Moira Stanley, eds., *A Punishment in Search of a Crime*. New York: Avon Books, 1989. Members of the civil rights group Amnesty International, Gray and Stanley present various essays arguing against the death penalty.

Marianne LeVert, *Crime*. New York: Facts On File, 1991. This book for young people offers an overview of the causes of crime and society's attempts to promote lawful behavior.

Tamara L. Roleff, ed., *Police Brutality*. San Diego, CA: Greenhaven Press, 1999. This book for young people offers a collection of essays related to the issue of police brutality.

Samuel Walker, *Popular Justice: A History of American Criminal Justice*. New York: Oxford University Press, 1980. For more advanced readers, this book presents a history of the American criminal justice system, emphasizing the problems the country has had in meeting public demands while maintaining the rule of law.

WORKS CONSULTED

Associated Press, "Gun-Control Advocates Seize School Shootings to Push for New State, National Laws," *Dallas Morning News,* June 7, 1998. This Associated Press news report discusses the drive to create new gun control laws in America in the aftermath of several school shootings.

Associated Press, "High Court Upholds California's 3-Strikes Law," *Dallas Morning News,* January 20, 1999. This news report talks about a U.S. Supreme Court ruling upholding California's three-strikes law.

Associated Press, "Study: Inmates Serving More Time: Government Cites State Law Targeting Violent Offenders," *Dallas Morning News,* January 11, 1999. This news report offers statistics regarding the amount of time people spend in prison nationwide.

Associated Press Online, "Judge: Cookie Thief Must Serve 'Three-Strikes' Sentence," March 15, 1998. This Associated Press release reports that a judge upheld a sentence of twenty-five years to life in prison for stealing four cookies.

John S. Baker Jr., "Federalization of Criminal Law," congressional testimony, May 6, 1999. An expert in criminal law, Baker testified before Congress regarding the trend towards giving more power to the federal government to control crime, as well as the concept of a national police force.

Scott Baldauf, "Death Row Has Its Own Gender Gap," *Christian Science Monitor,* January 23, 1998. Reporter Scott Baldauf discusses the controversy surrounding the execution of Karla Faye Tucker.

Sandy Banks, "Life as We Live It: Did Tucker Really Deserve Our Pity?" *Los Angeles Times*, February 6, 1998. Reporter Sandy Banks discusses the fair application of the death penalty in light of the Karla Faye Tucker case.

Michael Barone, "More Guns, Less Crime?" *Public Interest*, October 15, 1998. A senior staff editor at *Reader's Digest*, Barone discusses John Lott's book *More Guns, Less Crime*, which suggests that crime rates will go down if more people own guns.

Bob Barr, "Gun Laws Don't Work," a sidebar within Patricia V. Rivera's article "Gun Laws Don't Work," *USA Today*, December 19, 1995. As chairman of the House Firearms Legislation Task Force, Republican congressman Bob Barr expresses his opposition to gun control legislation.

Georgette Bennett, *Crime Warps: The Future of Crime in America.* New York: Anchor Books, 1989. Criminologist Georgette Bennett uses crime statistics to predict future trends in crime.

Linda Bernard, "Michigan Speaks with a Forked Tongue on Youth Issues," *Michigan Chronicle,* June 16, 1998. Attorney Linda Bernard criticizes the state of Michigan for cutting programs and services related to the physical and psychological well-being of children.

Paul Braun, "Freedom at Risk," letter to the editor, *Ventura County Star*, July 11, 1999. This letter argues against new gun control laws.

Judy Briscoe, "Breaking the Cycle of Violence: A Rational Approach to At-Risk Youth," *Federal Probation*, September 1, 1997. This lengthy article discusses juvenile crime prevention, and is based on a presentation that crime expert Judy Briscoe made to the United Nations in June 1997.

Scott Burger, "Controlling Criminals, Not Guns, Prevents Trouble," *Rocky Mountain Collegian/University Wire,* October 1, 1998. Burger expresses his opposition to gun control laws.

Christian Science Monitor, "Bulging Prisons: Editorials," August 21, 1998. This editorial argues that it is more important to spend money on rehabilitating prisoners than on locking them up.

John Cloud, with reporting by Harriet Barovick, Cathy Booth, and

Sylvester Monroe, "Crime: For They Know Not What They Do?" *Time*, August 24, 1998. *Time* magazine's reporters discuss the inability of juvenile criminals to understand the consequences of their crimes.

John Cloud, with reporting by Andrew Goldstein, Elaine Rivera, Viveca Novak, Elaine Shannon, and Kermit Pat, "Law: A Get-Tough Policy That Failed," *Time*, February 1, 1999. *Time* magazine's reporters criticize mandatory sentencing laws.

Richard Cohen, "Poverty Can Be Fatal Mistake," *St. Louis Post-Dispatch*, March 17, 1994. Richard Cohen of the *Washington Post* Writers Group discusses the unfair application of the death penalty.

Rhonda Cook, "Three Strikes, You're Broke," *Atlanta Constitution*, November 13, 1998. Cook discusses the cost of enforcing three-strikes laws in relation to their effectiveness.

John Donvan, Ted Koppel, "The Abner Louima Case," *ABC Nightline,* February 26, 1998. This television program examines an incidence of police brutality in New York.

Barbara Dority, "More Power, Less Responsibility," *Humanist*, September 19, 1998. This article discusses a U.S. Supreme Court ruling related to the responsibility of police regarding deaths that occur during high-speed chases.

Economist, "The Police: Excessive Force," July 11, 1998. This article reports on complaints by the Human Rights Group about police brutality.

Christopher John Farley and James Willwerth, "Dead Teen Walking," *Time*, January 19, 1998. This article discusses the possible innocence of Shareef Cousin, a juvenile currently on death row.

Samuel D. Faulkner and Larry P. Danaher, "Controlling Subjects: Realistic Training vs. Magic Bullets," *FBI Law Enforcement Bulletin*, February 1, 1997. Faulkner teaches law enforcement techniques at the Ohio Peace Officer Training Academy in Columbus, Ohio; Danaher is a lieutenant with the Lafayette, Indiana, Police Department. Their article discusses various methods of controlling subjects who are resisting arrest.

Gary Fields, "Will New Gun Checks Misfire? State Record-Keeping Is System's Achilles' Heel," *USA Today*, November 30, 1998. Fields reports on problems with the newest version of the Brady Law.

Alison Fitzgerald, "Killer Wants to Become Police Officer," *Los Angeles Times*, June 22, 1997. Fitzgerald reports on the case of Hassan Smith, who killed a man as a juvenile and wants to become a police officer.

Gilbert G. Gallegos, "Human Rights Group's Police-Brutality Claim Unfounded," *USA Today*, October 14, 1998. National president of the Fraternal Order of Police in Washington, D.C., Gilbert Gallegos criticizes an Amnesty International report that suggests police brutality is widespread in America.

David Gelernter, "What Do Murderers Deserve?" *Commentary*, April 1, 1998. David Gelernter is a professor of computer science at Yale who was letter bombed and seriously injured in June 1993; he argues that the death penalty is necessary in a civilized society.

Stefanie Grant, "A Dialogue of the Deaf? New International Attitudes and the Death Penalty in America," *Criminal Justice Ethics*, June 22, 1998. An expert in the criminal justice system discusses international attitudes towards America's application of the death penalty.

Sara Jean Green, "Police Need Guns, Juries Told," *Toronto Star*, March 4, 1999. This brief article discusses the necessity of guns in police work.

Ira J. Hadnot, "John Lott Jr.: Interview," *Dallas Morning News*, May 31, 1998. Using a question-and-answer format, Hadnot reports on an interview with John Lott, the author of a controversial book on gun control.

Lee Hancock, "Death Sentence Debate Centers on Gender," *Dallas Morning News*, January 25, 1998. Reporter Lee Hancock discusses the controversy surrounding the execution of Karla Faye Tucker.

Sean Hannity and Alan Colmes, "Los Angeles Shootings," *Hannity and Colmes*, Fox News Network, August 11, 1999. In discussing a violent shooting in Los Angeles, California, two talk show hosts examine issues related to gun control in America.

Susan N. Herman, "Prisons Aren't for Young Offenders," *Newsday*, July 8, 1997. A professor at Brooklyn Law School, Herman argues that juvenile criminals should not be housed in adult prisons.

Seth Hettena, "Experts Challenge GOP Candidate's Boast That 'Three Strikes' Reduces Crime," Associated Press Online, October 25, 1998. Hettena reports on criticisms of California's three-strikes law.

Renee Schafer Horton, "Celebrating Death: Public Reaction to Tucker Execution Is Disquieting," *Dallas Morning News*, February 15, 1998. A freelance writer, Horton criticizes people who celebrate whenever the death penalty is enacted.

Carl Ingram, "Wilson Proposes Overhaul of Juvenile Justice System," *Los Angeles Times*, April 10, 1997. Ingram reports on a California governor's suggestion that the minimum age for the death penalty be lowered from eighteen to fourteen.

Inter Press News Service English Newswire, "Jamaica: Government Moves to Halt Bloody Crime Wave," July 15, 1999. This news release reports on the Jamaican government's efforts to confiscate privately owned guns.

Tom Jarriel, Hugh Downs, and Barbara Walters, "He's Only a Child," *ABC 20/20*, February 13, 1998. This television program reports on the Nathaniel Abraham murder case.

John Jenswold, "Big Prisons Won't End Crime," *Madison (WI) Capital Times*, May 21, 1998. Jenswold argues that building more prisons and locking offenders up for longer periods of time will not decrease crime in America.

Dane M. Johnston, "The Unforgiven," letter to the editor, *Utne Reader*, June 1999. This letter criticizes the ideas of David Gelernter, who argues in favor of the death penalty.

Sylvia Kinyoun, "Wise Founders," letter to the editor, *Ventura County Star*, July 11, 1999. This letter argues against new gun control legislation.

Ted Koppel, "The Blue Wall," *ABC Nightline*, August 21– 22, 1997. This television special discusses the Louima police brutality case in depth.

Arlene Levinson, "Wrongly Accused Find Themselves at Death's Door," (Vancouver, WA) *Columbian*, November 11, 1998. Associated Press reporter Arlene Levinson discusses several cases where innocent people have been released from death row shortly before their executions.

Paul D. Linnee, "Limit Police Pursuit and Bad Guys Will Escape," *Minneapolis Star Tribune*, December 19, 1998. This article by a former police officer argues that police should be given the power to pursue criminals in high-speed chases.

John R. Lott Jr., "Concealed Guns Reduce Crime; If People Are Packing, Crooks Think Twice," *Minneapolis Star Tribune*, August 16, 1998. A professor of law and economics at the University of Chicago, Lott uses FBI crime studies to conclude that crime would be reduced if more law-abiding citizens carry guns.

Bo Lozoff, "The Unforgiven," letter to the editor, *Utne Reader*, June 1999. Author expresses the view that criminals deserve to be treated as human beings.

Brett Mahoney and Asha Blake, "Crime and Punishment for Children," *ABC World News This Morning*, March 26, 1998. This news program discusses the juvenile justice system.

Deborah Mathis and Chris Collins, "Jonesboro Attack Leaves Many Questions on Children, Justice," Gannett News Service, April 4, 1998. This article discusses laws and policies related to the automatic release of juvenile prisoners upon adulthood.

Dan McGraw, "When Is Forgiveness Unforgivable?" *U.S. News & World Report*, February 9, 1998. Reporter Dan McGraw discusses the Karla Faye Tucker death penalty case.

Antonio Mora and Kevin Newman, "Justice for Juveniles," *ABC Good Morning America*, March 27, 1998. This television program discusses the issue of trying juveniles as adults.

Richard Moran and Bob Edwards, "High-Speed Chases," *Morning*

Edition, National Public Radio, October 14, 1997. This discussion between radio host Bob Edwards and professor of sociology and criminology Richard Moran examines various issues related to the dangers and necessity of high-speed police chases.

New Republic, "Rusty Got His Gun," August 17, 1998. This editorial advocates stricter gun control laws.

Sam Newlund, "High-Speed Police Chases Are a Risky Business That We'd Do Better to Ban," *Minneapolis Star Tribune*, May 12, 1996. This article argues that the government should ban high-speed police chases because they are too dangerous to individual safety.

Susan Nielsen, "Only Ugly Male Atheists Deserve to Die, Right?" *Columbian*, February 5, 1998. Reporter Susan Nielsen discusses the unsuccessful movement to pardon Karla Faye Tucker, who was executed for murder.

Emanuel Parker, "'3 Strikes Bad, Costly, Ineffective': County Public Defender," *Los Angeles Sentinel,* April 26, 1995. Parker reports on criticisms of California's three-strikes law by Los Angeles County public defender Michael P. Judge.

Marie-Claire Perrault, "The Unforgiven," letter to the editor, *Utne Reader*, June 1999. This letter criticizes the ideas of David Gelernter, who argues in favor of the death penalty.

Anthony J. Pinizzotto, Edward F. Davis, and Charles E. Miller III, "In the Line of Fire: Learning from Assaults on Law Enforcement Officers," *FBI Law Enforcement Bulletin*, February 1, 1998. Pinizzotto and Davis teach behavioral sciences at the FBI Academy in Quantico, Virginia; Miller teaches in the education/training services unit at the FBI's criminal justice information services division in Clarksburg, West Virginia. Their article reports on a study of officers who have been assaulted on the job.

Eric Pooley et al., "Crime and Punishment: Death or Life? McVeigh Could Be the Best Argument for Executions, but His Case Highlights the Problems That Arise When Death Sentences Are Churned Out in Huge Numbers," *Time,* June 16, 1997. This article not only offers a lengthy discussion of capital punishment but also includes statistics and the results of public opinion polls on the issue.

William Raspberry, "We Too Easily Overlook Some Violations," *Dallas Morning News,* October 13, 1998. *Washington Post* reporter William Raspberry discusses an Amnesty International report on police brutality in America.

Dean Reynolds and Ted Koppel, "The Troubling Case of Karla Faye Tucker," *ABC Nightline,* February 3, 1998. This television program presents an interview with Karla Faye Tucker, then on death row pending execution, as well as interviews with people involved with her case.

Lisa Richardson, "Activists Seek to Limit Three-Strikes Law Sentencing," *Los Angeles Times*, August 17, 1998. Staff writer Lisa Richardson discusses the activities of a group called Families to Amend Three Strikes, which seeks to eliminate long sentences for drug users and dealers.

Warren Richey, "High Court Expands Police Power to Search," *Christian Science Monitor,* April 7, 1999. This article reports on the broadening of police powers regarding search-and-seizure laws.

Harold J. Rothwax, *Guilty: The Collapse of Criminal Justice.* New York: Warner Books, 1996. Rothwax criticizes many aspects of the American judicial system, using examples from his twenty-five years as a judge.

Herbert A. Sample, "Police Chase Ends in High Court," *Denver Rocky Mountain News*, December 8, 1997. This article reports on the result of a U.S. Supreme Court ruling related to a death that occurred during a high-speed police chase.

Stephanie Saul, "Adult Punishment: Minors Face Death Row for Crimes," *Newsday,* March 3, 1997. In discussing the trial of a seventeen-year-old murderer in Mississippi, reporter Stephanie Saul examines the issue of juveniles on death row.

William A. Schroeder, "When Death Is a Just Punishment," *St. Louis Post-Dispatch,* June 12, 1994. Reporter William Schroeder suggests that the death penalty be limited to multiple murderers and serial killers.

Robert Siegel, host, "Two Decades Later, Americans Divided over Death Penalty," *All Things Considered*, National Public Radio, July 2, 1996. Robert Siegel interviews several experts on the death penalty and discusses public opinions on the issue.

Tony Snow, "Capital Punishment: Most Arguments Against It Don't Hold Up," *Dallas Morning News*, February 5, 1998. *Detroit News* columnist Tony Snow argues in favor of capital punishment.

Ray Suarez, "Jonesboro Convictions," *Talk of the Nation*, National Public Radio, August 12, 1998. This radio program offers expert opinions about issues related to juvenile crime, particularly murder.

Ray Suarez, "Kids and Gun Violence," *Talk of the Nation*, National Public Radio, March 31, 1998. This interview features prominent speakers on both sides of the gun control issue.

Ray Suarez, "Preventing Juvenile Crime," *Talk of the Nation*, National Public Radio, April 15, 1998. This interview features speakers who deal with juvenile crime prevention and related issues.

Ray Suarez, "Victims' Rights," *Talk of the Nation*, National Public Radio, July 7, 1998. This interview features experts in victims' rights as well as defense attorneys, both of whom argue about whether criminal rights should be given as much weight as victims' rights.

Josh Sugarman, "Reverse Fire: The Brady Bill Won't Break the Sick Hold Guns Have on America. It's Time for Tougher Measures," *Mother Jones*, January 1, 1994. Sugarman advocates banning private handgun ownership in America.

Jacob Sullum, "Weapon Assault: The Advantage of Weak Arguments," *Reason*, July 1, 1994. Sullum argues that limited gun bans will quickly lead to far-reaching ones, thereby infringing on an individual's right to own a gun.

Tampa Oracle, "Editorial: Miranda Rights Serve Purpose," University Wire, February 16, 1999. This editorial argues in favor of maintaining the current status of Miranda warnings, which mandate that police must tell suspects they have the right to remain silent.

William Tucker, "Unbroken Windows: The Good News on Crime," *American Spectator*, March 1, 1998. This lengthy article discusses various reasons for crime increases and decreases and offers support for the death penalty.

USA Today, "Adult Time for Adult Crime? 'Blending' Is a Better Way," March 30, 1998. This editorial advocates blending juvenile and adult sentences for serious crimes.

Rick Van Sant, "Cost of Police Chases Too High," *Denver Rocky Mountain News*, August 30, 1998. Van Sant argues that police should not be allowed to pursue minor criminals in high-speed automobile chases because these chases are too dangerous.

Washington Transcript Service, "U.S. Representative Charles Schumer (D-NY) Holds News Conference on Gun Control," May 22, 1998. As the ranking Democrat on the Crime Committee of New York, Schumer advocates making it mandatory for guns to have trigger locks.

Washington Transcript Service, "U.S. Senator Barbara Boxer (D-CA) Holds News Conference to Discuss Brady Law Implementation," November 30, 1998. Senator Boxer discusses mandatory waiting periods for gun buyers, as well as other aspects of the Brady Law.

Charlie Weaver, "Violent Youth Must Get Clear Message: You'll Be Held Accountable," *Minneapolis Star Tribune*, February 5, 1998. Representative Charlie Weaver of Minnesota argues that violent juvenile offenders need to be tried as adults.

Henry Weinstein, "3-Strikes Law Overstated, Study Says," *Los Angeles Times*, October 11, 1998. *Times* legal affairs writer Henry Weinstein discusses whether or not California's three-strikes law actually reduces crime.

Linda Wertheimer, host, "Three Strikes Law Packs Jails in California," *All Things Considered*, National Public Radio, September 30, 1994. This radio program discusses California's three-strikes law and the problems involved with enforcing it.

Diane Whiteley, "The Victim and the Justification of Punishment," *Criminal Justice Ethics*, June 22, 1998. An expert in criminal justice, Whiteley discusses society's reasons for punishing individual wrongdoers.

James Q. Wilson, "Restoring Sanity to a Criminal Justice System Gone Astray," *Washington Times*, April 12, 1998. Wilson discusses Susan Estrich's 1998 book *Getting Away with Murder: How Politics Is Destroying the Criminal Justice System*, which advocates eliminating mandatory sentencing laws.

James Q. Wilson and Susanne Washburn, "A Rhythm to the Madness," *Time*, August 23, 1993. This brief article blames increases in crime partly on increases in individual rights.

Wisconsin State Journal, "Capital Punishment: It's the Wrong Answer," October 17, 1993. This editorial argues against the death penalty, listing several reasons why it is an ineffective approach to reducing crime.

Jonathan Wright, "Rights Group Says Police Brutality Rife in U.S.," Reuters, July 7, 1998. Jonathan Wright's news report discusses accusations by an American human rights group that there is widespread police brutality in the United States.

Dave Zweifel, "After 2 Years, No Justice in '3 Strikes,'" *Madison (WI) Capital Times*, March 13, 1996. Zweifel discusses flaws in California's three-strikes law.

Index

106

PICTURE CREDITS

Cover photo: PhotoDisc

AFP/Corbis, 28, 31, 77

Associated Press, 19, 21, 45, 68

Bettmann/Corbis, 12

Donna Binder/Impact Visuals, 29, 31

Ron Chapple/FPG International, 17

Mike Derer/AP, 15

PhotoDisc, 10, 57, 80

Jack Plunkett/AP, 69

Paul Sakuma/AP, 58

C. Takagi/Impact Visuals, 39, 46

Nik Wheeler/Corbis, 42

Max Whittaker/AP, 64

Jeff Zelevansky/AP, 40

About the Author

Patricia D. Netzley received her bachelor's degree in English from the University of California at Los Angeles (UCLA). After graduation she worked as an editor at the UCLA Medical Center, where she produced hundreds of medical articles, speeches, and pamphlets.

Netzley became a freelance writer in 1986. She is the author of several books for children and adults, including *The Assassination of President John F. Kennedy* (Macmillan/New Discovery Books, 1994), *Alien Abductions* (Greenhaven Press, 1996), *Issues in the Environment* (Lucent Books, 1998), and the forthcoming *Encyclopedia of Environmental Literature* (ABC-CLIO).

Netzley's hobbies are weaving, knitting, and needlework. She and her husband, Raymond, live in Southern California with their three children, Matthew, Sarah, and Jacob.